The
Three-Day Departure
of
Mrs. Annette Zinn

A Novel
Mary E. Carter

THE
THREE-DAY DEPARTURE
of
MRS. ANNETTE ZINN

A NOVEL

Mary E. Carter

From the award-winning author of the novel
I, Sarah Steinway
2018 National Jewish Book Awards FINALIST Debut Fiction
2018 New Mexico-Arizona Book Awards WINNER Best Religious Book

TOVAH
MIRIAM

Cover and photographs on pages 3, 47, 139: ShutterStock

All other photographs and paintings © 2019 Mary E. Carter

MARY E. CARTER

ISBN 978-0-578-52193-0

First Printing

TOVAH
MIRIAM

www.Tovah-Miriam.com

Neither Forgotten nor Hidden

Bea and Joel

May their memories be a blessing.

"And the almond blossoms,
     and the locust tree is laden,
     and the caper fruit falls apart.

For man is going to his everlasting house,
and the mourners turn round in the market.

Until the silver cord is snapped,
     and the golden bowl is smashed,
     and the pitcher is broken against the well,
     and the jug smashed at the pit.

And dust returns to the earth as it was,
and the life-breath returns to God Who gave it.

Merest breath, said Qohelet. All is mere breath."

—Qohelet 12: 5-8

Stones have no agency.

They survive in colonies of other stones.
They are buried under mountains.
They fall, shaken, by earthquakes.
They are scooped up by bulldozers, crushed to become gravel,
blown to bits in war, brutally mined, and made into wedding rings.
Then, one day, a stone lands in sunlight.
A glint of pyrite on the stone's surface catches the eye.
The stone is slung into a denim pocket.
Later, fingers draw it out of the denim darkness.
It is placed, ceremonial, among other stones.

Rocks, pebbles, stones – they have no agency.

Day One

Henry Preston pads into Mrs. Zinn's cozy library. He senses it immediately. Things are out of alignment. The windows, clothed in layers of lace and velveteen, still embrace the morning sunshine. But it's all wrong. It's off, somehow.

Ah.

Yes.

Oh, dear.

"Mrs. Zinn?"

He touches her shoulder.

"Annette?"

She is still warm.

"Oh dear. Dear, dear Mrs. Zinn. Oh, Annette. What have you gone and done?"

At ninety-five, it is unlikely that she has *done* anything other than to yield, then to slip, into the world to come.

May her memory be for a blessing.

Henry is not surprised, yet he is startled. The morning sun beams across Mrs. Zinn's blond waves.

Mrs. Annette Zinn, A-Double-N, E-Double-T-E. She had always introduced herself that way – has died.

She is hovering near the ceiling of her library right now.

She is seated in her usual chair. She is leaning forward a bit at the waist as if listening to someone in the other chair. But her chin lolls toward her chest. Her breakfast tray rests on the footstool. Her morning tea, now dregs, sits alongside her silver toast caddy. Three triangles of toast stand at the ready. Her starched linen napkin is folded into the shape of a swan. It floats on the corner of her tray.

That's how Annette floats, right now. Well, it's not floating, exactly. Hovering more like. She is hovering near the ceiling of her library right now. Annette discovers that she can rise above, and yet remain connected to, the scene below. Apparently, the world to come is much like the world as it has always been. She is surprised by this. Floating, she is surprised. She can see and hear everyone and everything, and yet she is no longer able to participate in things. She cannot speak nor act upon any of the activities down there. And, surprisingly, she has little urge to do so. She feels remote. She feels detached. And, of course, she is detached. And it is not a bad feeling at all. On the contrary, she feels free, liberated perhaps. It's a good feeling. She is here and not here, aware, but not involved. She can witness but not intervene. She is absolved of her presence in life.

Well. Well.

She observes Henry now.

Henry crouches on the carpet next to Mrs. Zinn's chair and, kneeling there, he looks up into her face. Her glasses are askew. Henry gentles them back onto the bridge of her nose. The little gold chain that attaches to the temples is a bit twisted. He sorts it out.

Now Henry needs to let the household know what has happened. Grunting a little, favoring a bad left knee, he gets up and slips his cellphone out of his pocket and swipes. He needs to get everyone moving along. There is much to do, as usual. Only today, it's different. Not unrehearsed. Just different. Henry recites to himself the list of things to do:

"We need to call Mrs. Rothenberg. We need to call Irene and Doug – Douglas. We need to call the Dempseys. And Rabbi Blackburn. Call Hillside. They know what to do. We need to get her ready. Take the good necklaces and these earrings . . ."

He touches them gently on her still-warm earlobes:

". . . and put them in the safe."

In his book, *The Soul*, Rabbi Adin Even Israel Steinsaltz states:

> *"In the corpus of Jewish mystical literature, it is said that for three days after the death of the body, the soul is still hovering close to the body, so to speak, and does not completely depart from it. In short, the soul requires some time to accustom itself to its new situation."*

Mrs. Zinn wonders:

"How on earth can I remember this, right now, floating, as I am, up here? Perhaps I should have paid more attention to that book. Maybe that way, I would have been more prepared for what is happening to me right now."

In *The Soul*, the rabbi continues:

> *"After the soul departs from the body, it undergoes a process of rectification . . . this process is known in the kabbalistic literature as the "hollow of a sling". Simply put, this is the most comprehensive overview possible of our lives in this world; it is*

For three days after the death of the body, the soul is still hovering close to the body.

similar to the old saying that, "when you die, your whole life passes before your eyes."

. . . In the "hollow of a sling" the soul . . . apprehends the whole of its former life process at once . . . The soul acquires a certain comprehension of the details of events that were forgotten or hidden during its time in the world."

What **forgotten** events? How can Mrs. Zinn comprehend forgotten events?

Which **hidden** events? How can Mrs. Zinn perceive hidden events?

How can she begin to comprehend things that are forgotten or hidden? How does this work? It's impossible.

Now that she is about to enter the world to come, will she be able to comprehend even the hidden or forgotten details from her time in this world?

Perhaps now, from this strange new vantage point, her task is to piece it all together to make her life *whole*. Homework, so to speak, now that she is in the home stretch.

Will her whole life pass before her eyes? Her life, *whole*?

What
forgotten *events?*

Which
hidden *events?*

Mrs. Zinn wonders:

Is, was, this now, or then?
Am I, or was I, here, or there, then or now?
Was that then, or is this now?
Was that me, or is this me, now?
Where am, or was, I?
Is this now, or then, or when?
If not now, when?
I am, or was, so confused.
Am I here?
Or there?
Or where?
Is this now?
Or then?
Did this happen?
Or is this happening?
How can I see without having seen?
How now?
But not then?
I am so confused.
Was I always so confused?
Will I be thus, further, confused?
Where am I?
Here or there?
Or nowhere?
Am I lost?
Forgotten?
Both?
Neither?

*H*enry Preston has worked in Mrs. Zinn's household for more than twenty-five years, progressing from favored lunch companion, to fond friend, then on to confidant. Finally Mrs. Zinn had asked him if he would like to join her household to be chief-of-staff, or aid-de-camp, or butler.

"Do people say butler anymore?" she had asked him rhetorically, a touch of irony in her voice. They had giggled at that, rueful.

She had asked him to join her, and to help her, and to be her companion. This project could be fun for Henry Preston at his age; he had just turned fifty-two. He and Mrs. Zinn were well matched; quite well suited, always comfortable with one another. Almost like spouses. But much, much better, yes? They had laughed at that one. Yes, much, much better than spouses.

And, yes, it had seemed to be a good idea to both of them. Thus, he had boarded her luxurious little vessel and commenced upon his duties to keep order with things and with people in Mrs. Zinn's world.

Now, from the kitchen, Henry hears the clatter of china tea things being set down, a bit too abruptly. Floating up there, Mrs. Zinn hears it too. Can't they handle the china without crashing it around?

Then, quickly, quickly, the big pivot door flaps open, banging against the wainscot. And quickly, house slippers muffle across the living room carpet. It is Mrs. Etabari, Annette's nurse, summoned by Henry's text message. She presses into Henry's side as he recites this day's instructions to her:

"Give her the costume pieces for removal. And dress her in the peach linen. And don't forget the rings, her rings. Put the jewelry she's wearing now in the blue draw-string bag, and put it in the safe, second shelf down."

Henry keys in two more text messages – to Mrs. Zinn's driver and the chef. Then, taking the elevator instead of his usual route up the stairs, he approaches her desk. He knows where to look, what to do, and he proceeds with his usual tact and deliberation. Mrs. Zinn had often said to anyone who would listen:

"I found this marvelous man."

Mrs. Zinn had said this. Many times. Not just once. She had said this, even to Henry himself:

"I found this marvelous man."

Now she watches this marvelous man, viewing him as she bobs gently from the ceiling of her library. She feels like a birthday balloon; not an unpleasant sensation. Festive almost, happy too.

"Oh, Henry. You are so good."

She bobs gently from the ceiling of her library.

$\mathscr{T}$hen, as if on cue, a spotlight snaps on, bright and clear and stark, illuminating to Mrs. Zinn, hidden events from Henry's life:

In honor of Henry's fiftieth birthday, a costume party had been organized. He had dressed as Keith Richards, tied a bandana around his head, scrunched up his hair into an artful mess, and tossed on a tank top.

During the festivities, Henry-Keith decided he liked a young man who was dressed as a pirate. The young pirate wore a fetching black eye-patch and full-length black leather pirate boots with flaring folded cuffs and brass buckles.

Arriving back at his house, with his dashing new friend, Henry watched pirate-boy touring the great room, and the library, and the great mahogany dining room with its silver hollowware and its collection of English china teapots. The boy seemed to possess a discerning eye. As he strided past Henry's Paul Revere coffee pot, for example, he touched it lightly with a long and covetous finger-tip. He bent forward, flipping the eyepatch up, to get a closer look at the signature on a gold-framed oil painting. He caressed Henry's stone

In honor of Henry's fiftieth birthday, a costume party had been organized. He had dressed as Keith Richards.

—17—

Buddha. And an Acoma pot. He reverently turned over the 1824 silver commemorative trowel, rubbing a thumb over the engraving on both sides of it. His appreciation for Henry's treasures was sensual and lingering.

Twenty-five years ago, Henry Preston and Mrs. Annette Zinn met in the auction rooms at Butterfield's.

Lately, Henry had been a fixture at Christie's and Sotheby's, and at many other auction houses. He had been working conscientiously on restoring his household treasures since the "incident." Mrs. Zinn had noted that he could discern a "find from a fraud" at a sale and, later on, she would discover that Henry could even turn his skills to the evaluation of people. Because of his experience with pirate-boy, Henry could discern the nuances of fraudulence in people as well as in antiquities. But, of course, when he and Mrs. Zinn met, she could not have known how he had honed that particular skill.

Now Mrs. Zinn is Henry's witness. Really, right now, she had no choice but to watch this hidden event from Henry's life:

Fiendish, swift, without a word, the young man struck Henry, hard, several times, in the ribs, with both fists, he knocked the wind out of Henry. Then pirate-boy smashed his fist into Henry's cheek. He kicked him across his femur and in the belly, many loud kicks with his pirate boots. The boy was strong, unrelenting. He no sooner landed a blow than he struck again, catching Henry in freefall to strike, again and again, upwards under Henry's jaw, downwards across the back of Henry's neck.

Then, quick, efficient, the kid rolled Henry, tight, into one of Henry's finest Bokharas. That rug resided on the polished oak of the great room floor. He rolled Henry across the great room like a human cigar. Bleeding, and bruised, and not quite dead, Henry watched as pirate-boy commenced upon a burglary, a desecration, of Henry's entire house, right in front of Henry's eyes as blood seeped into the rug. This boy was a real-life pirate. A young man in a pirate costume. It was ridiculous. A horror. A cheap joke. A cliché.

From her new vantage point, Mrs. Zinn could now see the places and the people who had been in her world, her life. Suddenly Mrs. Zinn sees into the past. She sees herself in her own past and she sees Henry's past too:

Mrs. Zinn had not known about that terrible incident in Henry's life. Henry had never told her about it. He had hinted at it when he was in one of his black moods. But she had never prodded. She simply let him talk. Or not talk. And he had not talked about that.

Do I really want to know the truths behind everyone and everything?

This life review may turn out to be painful. Worse. Excruciating.

Well. Well.

She had
never prodded.
She simply
let him talk.

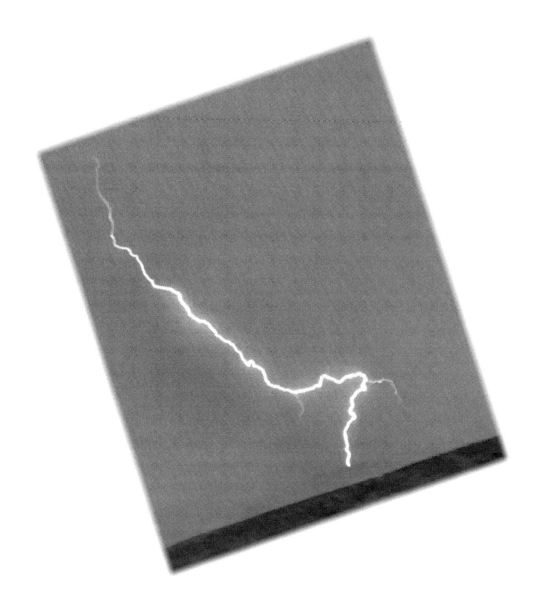

*M*rs. Zinn watches, horrified, as Henry's ordeal unfolds:

The lad worked methodically, wrapping delicate treasures in table cloths, and napkins, and dish towels. He placed objects into black plastic garbage bags, arranging them rather carefully. He was tidy. He had all the time in the world as Henry faded in and out of consciousness. Then pirate-boy hoisted his booty, up and over his shoulders, and took it out the back door that opened onto Henry's three-car garage. Woozy and coming around for a moment, Henry witnessed as the lad swiped the car keys off the entry hall console. Later, Henry would discover that one of the cars was missing.

Throughout the pillaging, Henry listened to the clinks and clunks of things being removed from his rooms. Later he would discover the extent of the losses. Pirate-boy had swung through the entire house, first downstairs, then upstairs – somewhat leisurely, he went through the whole house. Henry would discover that his pirate had also desecrated the place with piles of excrement here and there, where precious objects had once resided.

Then, without a word, his pirate left. He left Henry to – what? – to die? Probably. Who cared?

After the departure of the kid, Henry started the painful business of getting out of his trap. He rolled and strained inside his dense, heavy, and once-beloved Bokhara rug. Fuck the Bokhara. It was hard labor, excruciatingly painful, rolling and straining, squeezing himself out from the huge heavy rug. He had a broken rib; he was certain. One of Henry's ribs poked at an odd angle against the Keith Richards tank top. He was bleeding from his ear, from his head. Blood came from other wounds – he did not know where. With each breath, Henry gasped. In a perverse stroke of luck, the Keith Richards get-up, the bandana, had helped to keep blood from dripping into his eyes.

Finally, he rolled free enough to loosen the constriction of the rug, and he floundered out onto the hard-oak floor. He sat up. He managed to stand. He could walk, just.

Henry did not call 911. He did not call anybody.

Dizzy and nauseated, he staggered outside – his pirate

had left the garage door open. There was a can of paint, dripping at the edges, the lid thrown across the garage onto the cement floor, and a wet paintbrush thrown against the wall. One of the cars was missing, and there was an enormous splash of paint across the windshield of one of the other cars. As a matter of habit, of automatic, ridiculous, habitual fastidiousness, Henry pressed the button to close the huge garage door. That's when he saw that pirate-boy had signed his work. Using the old paint brush, dipped into the rich blue enamel of Henry's very own front door, pirate-boy had slopped his fare-thee-well onto the inside of the garage door:

HAPPY BIRTHDAY KEITH.

Henry shouted to the world:

"Gawd-dammed fucking son of a fucking fuck!"

Goodbye, pirate-boy.

Henry shouted, incoherently, shouted to the neighborhood, shouted to nobody, shouted to everybody:

"Fuck you, you fucking fuck! Just . . ."

He vomited onto his own foot.

Sobbing and bleeding and in so many kinds of pain that he could not have described what it was that he had felt at that moment, Henry folded down onto his knees, eased his arms around himself, embracing his chest, bending forward at his waist, and threw up again.

"God-damn-fucking son of a fuck."

Now hoarse, coughing phlegm, then spitting out a bloody tooth, and sobbing like he was thirteen years old on the junior high school playground, right here on his own driveway now, for all the world to see, his shrieks high-pitched:

". . . fucking fuck. You fucking fuckhead."

Nobody came to his aid. Nobody.

Henry would learn, later, that none of the neighbors had bothered to call the police. Don't get involved. It's a private matter. Domestic dispute.

And that is how it went.

Now Mrs. Zinn, anguished, knew.

It is too late, too late.

"Oh, Henry. You have been so good."

Well. Well.

Nobody came to his aid. Nobody.

At fifty, Henry turned his back on every thing and turned away from every one. From the hideous moment of being rolled into his own beloved rug, across the floor of his own beloved home, from that moment forward, he vowed:

"No more."

He made a vow.

Out of the echoes that sounded throughout his ruined house, he would clean up the messes and make a new life. He needed to rest. It was bad, the world. Worse than he had thought. Evil. People, who were the very devils incarnate, waited, threatening, just outside his own doorway. Never would he let them in again. Now he needed something. Maybe it was shelter from the storm, like Bob Dylan had said. Stupid. Stupid rock and roll. So corny. At this crossroads, he did not know exactly what it was he needed, but he was in desperate need.

"I found this marvelous man. His name is Henry Preston."

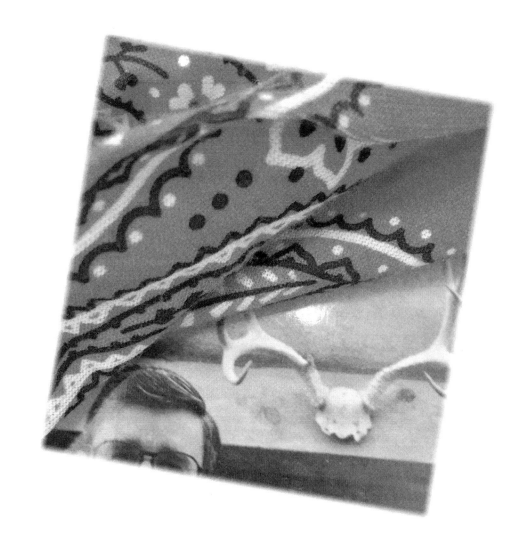

"No *more*."
He *made a vow*.

Henry liked to instruct Mrs. Zinn on the culture of the auction-hound. And Mrs. Zinn was an apt audience.

She was of a generation of women who looked up to men to be the leaders, in conversation, in knowledge, in wisdom, in business. She could not understand her younger women friends when they complained about "mansplaining." What was so bad about that? Mrs. Zinn paid attention and listened intently while Henry held forth on art and antiques and, later, as the years went by, she paid close attention to Henry when he held forth on people who came into Mrs. Zinn's circle.

"It is often the small item, Mrs. Zinn, the ignored and undervalued object, the orphaned desk or lamp, for example, that will turn out to be quite a find. Some treasures reside under the very noses of the regulars who habitually attend auctions. And even they will miss out on a very good bargain. You would think they would know better. For example: it can be a sadly undervalued catalog assessment of something that is determined to be out of fashion at the moment. To a discerning and experienced auction-hound, it may turn out to be the opportunity of a lifetime."

Henry did not exaggerate.

"For example, Mrs. Zinn, this tea set of yours."

He gestured to a silver tray with its tea pot, cups, saucers, and diminutive plates. He had discerned from her longing gaze and her notes in the margin of her catalog that Mrs. Zinn would make a bid. In effect, the tea set was already hers. Henry continued the lesson:

"These kinds of ladies' tea things have fallen from favor."

Turning a teacup over and examining the maker's mark on the bottom of the object, he observed:

"But they are nonetheless valuable even though they are currently undervalued. So, the alert buyer benefits from a fickle buying public.

And, just to illustrate what I am saying, Mrs. Zinn, I once discovered a very rare banjo clock in the most unostentatious consignment shop in Lomita. It was marked at nine hundred dollars. I asked the owner of the shop how he had found it, and he told me he had snapped it up it at an auction of household treasures, an estate sale. Which we should go to some time, by the way, Mrs. Zinn."

Encouraged by Mrs. Zinn's rapt attention, Henry summed up:

"Anyway, I knew for certain that it was worth at least ten thousand dollars. But such clocks were out of fashion at that moment. They were considered to be fusty, and most bargain hunters believed they were copies anyway. It looked to me like the shop owner was trying to turn this clock around quickly and for what he thought his market could bear. His price was actually a pittance. God knows what he paid for it at the estate sale. The clock was real. I could see that. So, I sped to the bank, got nine one-hundred-dollar bills, sped back to the shop, and the clock was mine. Later, at a more leisurely pace, I took it to Sotheby's for evaluation and, sure enough, they estimated it with an opening bid of nine thousand, five. It did well over twelve."

"Well. Well," Mrs. Zinn had said, giving him an appraising look. It would seem that Henry Preston might prove to be a knowledgeable and valuable companion.

As well he did.

And so, Mrs. Zinn and Henry Preston became regulars at the auction houses. They wandered around the pre-auction exhibitions and scoped out their prey. Henry was not at all shy about removing paintings from their hooks, peering at the backs of old canvases, tut-tutting sometimes, shaking his head dubiously:

"A very good approximation of a very good oil painting at a very good price, but it's a forgery. No earthly good to you, Mrs. Zinn."

And propping the unworthy picture against the floorboards of the auction showroom, he turned his back on it, bounding across the room to a rolled-up rug. He flapped the rug violently, unrolling it with a professional flourish, and flopped it onto the floor. Circling it, he flipped one corner of it into a triangle over the front of the rug:

"See, Mrs. Zinn. See how this side is so much more faded than the other side. It's not been turned properly. It's been allowed to sit beneath a south-facing window. I'd bet on it. Not worth a fraction of five thousand dollars at this point. But. If you like it, we could low-ball our bid. It might be nice over the back of a chair. It might be Navajo. It's not a good rug. But it may need a loving home."

This was how they spent their days, so many of their days, happy, happy days.

After the "incident," and a few months before Henry had met Mrs. Zinn, he had decided to start again to rebuild his personal collections. Then, once he had met Mrs. Zinn, both of them avid collectors, they got to work on their respective treasure hunts. They worked together in gentle companionship. Henry was searching for coins, paintings of the American West, English china, mahogany furniture – things like that. Gradually Henry restored sanity to his home, as he surrounded himself with items of cherished beauty. He indulged and nourished his senses by simply sitting, most evenings, in his favorite leather chair, a warm shade of brandy that pleased him enormously. He would sit there and contemplate the essences of the objects around him. His eyes caressed these lovely companions, and Henry was happy, simply imagining how these objects had traveled through time and across space, and he would often narrate to himself fanciful stories about the lives of these beautiful objects as they were moved from here to there and, finally, found their ways home to Henry.

And, in the same fanciful and serendipitous manner that these objects had traveled to Henry, Henry himself had traveled into Mrs. Zinn's household. Why and how he had accepted this late-life employment with Mrs. Zinn might well remain as much of a fantasy as why and how a silver charger now resided in his own vitrine.

Henry Preston was tasked with keeping Mrs. Zinn's home ship-shape, all the time. In addition to the items on Mrs. Zinn's to-do list, Henry had invented many other necessary tasks, and he saw to everything in the house and to everyone in Mrs. Zinn's employ, and he attended to it all, and to all of them, every day, often working well into the evenings. Henry never begrudged the long hours. He had made himself indispensable and adored by Mrs. Zinn. And he adored her, too. Every weekday he arrived at 7:30 AM and toiled, quietly and efficiently, and never rushing or pushy. He worked until "closing time," as they had dubbed it, around 8:00 PM. This employment would turn out to be the best job Henry had ever had.

Why would he have accepted this job at Mrs. Zinn's? He

was a man of means. He had retired – or been eased out of – a highly paid corporate advertising job as creative director of a large grey advertising agency. He owned a home on a fine and tree-lined street. His retirement package allowed him the means and the leisure to restructure – to rebuild – his own life.

Maybe for Henry, this job was safe harbor, shelter from the storm. Henry was meticulous about cornball associations, however, and he avoided simplistic wording for complex topics. And he loathed jargon, or idiom, or purloined bits of pop culture. He would have chosen better words to narrate the story of his employment with Mrs. Zinn. "Safe harbor" was not exactly correct. "Shelter from the storm" was a cliché. Yet the words somewhat satisfied Henry's sense of self, and those words were an appropriate tag line to his life story.

From the time he was twelve until his fiftieth birthday, Henry had inhabited a world of what, for him, had seemed to be nothing but a cacophony of indecipherable innuendo, obscure hints, and jokes. He was adrift among people who were arch, and camp, and uninhibited. He had eventually found himself a place in one of the most coveted of the cliques and, because he was unique, he became the "pet." He was genuinely innocent; no, he was a naïf. Thus, he was claimed by his companions, each one of whom cherished and wanted to protect Henry's innocence. Everybody loved Henry.

As did Mrs. Zinn.

*B*ack home, at Mrs. Zinn's after a day at the auctions, the two of them giggling and unwrapping their parcels, and draping them all over the library chairs, and arranging smaller items on the bookshelves, Henry would get on the phone and call Grace and Edith for a command performance:

"Come now! Come over at once! Come and see our new acquisitions!"

Mrs. Zinn, smiling and energized by their day's adventures, said:

"You are so good to me, Henry."

And her own goodness, which she bestowed upon Henry, times without number for twenty-five years, reverberated in Henry's memories, was a balm for him, had soothed him, time and again. May her memory be for a blessing; and it was to be.

And now she is gone.

Except Mrs. Zinn is not gone. She is here. How does this work, she wonders?

The rabbis had called it "the world to come," a euphemism for death she had supposed. But she had never given it much thought. She had never paid much attention to what those words might mean. Yes, she had attended lectures about Jewish mystical literature, the Zohar, and so forth. She had once even attended a workshop on Musar. But she was too earthbound to gather that information into her daily life. She had been tethered to this world, and she liked it that way. She needed to be bound in her temporal life. She was not curious about matters of the soul. She did not choose to go deeper into her own soul. She had been a realist.

But now she finds herself in this other world. She is floating above, seeing but not able to interact with anyone or anything. Now that she is a witness to things and events, some of which she could never have known about during her lifetime, she might have regretted not paying closer attention to mystical Jewish ideas and concepts. Except, in her present state, she had no regrets as such. She was not plagued by guilt or even by a sense of failure. Now she was simply the observer of her own life and of other people's lives. She could see things with more precision. Yes, precision. That was precisely the right word for how she saw things now in her new state of awareness. But what was this thing? What was happening to Annette Zinn right now?

She had questions. Or perhaps, a more precise word would be: reservations.

Since she had not known about Henry's abuse at the hands of the pirate-boy, and since, "your whole life passes before your eyes" – even including events that were forgotten or hidden from your living comprehension – wouldn't that mean, Annette wonders, would that not mean that her life had not been *whole*, but that it had been incomplete or even somewhat stunted? She felt – what was it she felt? – sad and humbled? Well, not precisely. There is that concept again, with its matching words: precise, precisely, precision. She did, however, realize, now, the things that she had not known – despite her long friendship with Henry – she had not ever truly known about Henry's reasons for being the way he was. His reasons for being in her life had been unknown to Annette.

Well. Well.

Ninety-five years was a good age. Now she is gone.

The downstairs bell rings, wafting shrill, through the rooms. Startled, Henry trots to get the door. It's Hillside. Two men have the gurney. It is discreetly covered with a checkered table cloth, of all things. They glide into the foyer. With solemn and deliberate motions, they approach Mrs. Zinn on her chair. And with practiced choreography, they lift her onto the gurney. It is all very quick. Very quiet.

As the removal proceeds, Henry stands next to what he and Mrs. Zinn had named "The Enormous Sofa." He clutches the edge of the sofa pillow with a little kneading motion of his thumb and fingers, back and forth, back and forth, along the welting. And if he is weeping, it is only evident by three muffled throat-clearing sounds and several squeaky gulps from beneath his turtleneck.

Mrs. Zinn, Annette, A-Double-N, E-Double-T-E, is leaving her home, her nest, her bit of heaven, her world while she was on this earth. Ninety-five years was a good age. Now she is gone.

Day Two

As the Hillside contingent rolled quietly out of the house, Henry thought that he'd better call Grace and Edith, himself, with the news:

"Hello, Mrs. Rothenberg? It's Henry."

"Oh, Henry. Yes? Oh, no! I can tell by your voice, Henry. When? How?"

"Some time this morning after she had had her tea. She also had eaten one piece of her toast. She was still warm when I came back into the library. Just sitting here, sort of sideways. Her glasses were crooked."

"Oh, Henry, you have been so good."

"Hillside came."

"Oh, Henry."

"They disguised the gurney with a table cloth!"

"No!"

"Red and white checks, like from an Italian restaurant."

"Oh, Henry. No! It's ludicrous. What can I say?"

"Yes."

"Oh, Henry. You have been so good."

"Well, Mrs. Rothenberg. We will miss our teas, won't we?"

"Oh, Henry," she had said, so many times, so many. "You are so good."

Henry had always been unpredictable when it came to setting out the tea things. One time for Mrs. Zinn and her girlfriends, Gracie and Edie, he made peanut butter and jelly tea sandwiches, and Grace burst out laughing as they each bit into their little bread triangles, and the jelly squeezed out the other side of the bread, and they had to lick their wrists, as the jelly forced them back into their girlhoods.

Then there was a silence as they each recalled childhood memories. They gripped their tea sandwiches, jelly still oozing along the edges:

"Who would have thought?"

"So much has happened."

"Look at us now."

And trailing off.

Three widows. Much bless-ed. And protected. Cosseted. And Mrs. Zinn the newest member of this little sorority. Gracie and Edie looked over at her. Their faces were reflected in the lenses of their glasses. The sun caught their rings, and their necklaces, and their polished nails. Mrs. Zinn spoke up:

"Well. A least I've got my own choppers!"

Grace expelled a great choking cough of a laugh. Then Edie chimed in with her unk, unk, unk, snort, snort, sort of laugh. And that started Mrs. Zinn into her nasal sniff, sniff, sniff, hack, screech laugh. And off they went. And someone dropped her tea sandwich onto her lap, and it was quite a little mess, and they just could not, could NOT, stop laughing.

Henry laughed too. You could not NOT laugh. But he kept in the background. Dealt discreetly with the sandwich crisis. Moved off back to the kitchen to get dessert – Girl Scout Cookies and Kool Aide. He was always creative that way.

Leaning back in her chair, Grace filled in a small silence:

"Not sure if I ever mentioned this: one day last year, right after I had pulled into the parking lot for my Torah study class, a car pulled into the space beside my car. I glanced to my left and saw this guy get out of his car. He

The sun caught their rings, and their necklaces, and their polished nails.

opened the rear door of his car, the one behind the driver's seat, and buckled up a big belt around his midsection. Then I saw him reach into the back seat, and he picked up a handgun and shoved it into the belt."

Annette, and Edie, and Henry, who had returned from the kitchen, were silent, and Grace continued:

"Without any hesitation, I got out of my car and walked right up to him and yelled, right in his face, "What are you DOING?" I used that tone of voice our mothers used, yelling at us when we were little, and we were about to do something stupid, or dangerous, or both. That tone of voice."

Her audience leaned forward a bit as Grace continued:

"I think our mother-voices strike a deep-seated memory in a man. I think grown-up men simply cannot abide that tone of voice. So, this guy, he drops what he's doing. He was about to reach into the back seat to get – and get this – to get another gun. A rifle or something. A long gun. Anyway, I'm right in his face again, and he starts talking, sort of stammering, and he asks me if I mind if he loads this other gun. Again, I yell, "YOU CAN'T DO THAT HERE. THIS IS A SYNAGOGUE."

Edie jumped in:

"Gracie! Don't ever do that again!"

"Well, honey, I can't honestly say that I won't do that again. Any more than I cannot slam on the brakes if a dog runs in front of my car. No, Edie. I can't promise I won't ever do that again."

There was a long silence while the three friends took it all in. Grace added, nonchalantly:

"Besides: I did not rationalize. I was NOT afraid. I just acted. I was acting on reflex."

Another silence.

"Turns out he was on some sort of supposed mission for the police department. I don't know. It was never explained to me very clearly by the sergeant that I reported the episode to."

Tikkun Olam.

Repair. Heal. Mend.

Make the world better.

Mrs. Annette Zinn had a laptop. Oh, yes. She used it

Tikkun Olam.
Repair. Heal. Mend.
Make the world better.

every day, even up to age ninety-five. In fact, she had been an early adopter when it came to digital technologies. She was an early adopter of every single digital gadget that came her way, throughout her latter years. This made her unique among her generation of widows. Grace and Edie lived contentedly without computers; "Feh," on the very idea! They would sit in Annette's library and tease her mercilessly as she clicked her way around the keys, googling this and googling that. She was very deft.

She placed her laptop on her lap (of course) most mornings and nestled into her favorite chair. There, along with her tea and toast and raspberry jam, and the morning sun beaming its way across her library carpet – there she clicked through her morning news. And, despite all the bad news, every once in a very great while, an item landed on her screen, good news, lovely news. Sometimes she would ask Henry to print something out. She needed to see it on paper. Although she was technologically very savvy, she was still of the generation that wanted to see her news in print.

Quickly, she googled: police, man with gun, and Grace's

synagogue name. There were a couple of items. Nothing conclusive. Edie scolded her:

"There you go again, Annette. Always poking around that infernal Internet."

Then, changing tack, Edie scolded again; this time, Grace's turn:

"Just don't do that. Ever again. Gracie. Just don't."

Grace shifted out of her shoes by using her big toes to shove them under the coffee table. She stretched her long legs out in front of herself with a cozy little squeal.

"I cannot swear, Edie, that I wouldn't do that ever again."

Annette had not thought about that story in years. Grace could have been shot. Murdered. Instead, she told the story, casually, as if the man with the gun had been just another everyday inconvenience. Always self-possessed and graceful, was Grace. How like Grace. Grace brought with her, everywhere she went, grace. And she would rest her graceful limbs and recite anecdotes, and Annette could draw grace around herself like a quilt. The friendships of the widows.

Then there was Edie.

Edie is what they used to call "a pistol." She had lived in the same college dorm as Annette during their freshman year. Their rooms opened onto an echoing, slightly dingy hallway. The curfew would strike before Edie, always late, thumped up the stairs, shrieking and laughing like a mad woman, and you couldn't help laughing too, she was that joyful. And drunken. The dorm "mother" stood with her wristwatch in her hand, dramatically peering at the timepiece, silently admonishing, then looking up, and through her thickish glasses, even as she could see that Edie was just so much fun. Staggering on the arms of her roommates, Edie railed about this and that, none of it intelligible, yet all of it uproariously funny. Standing in her doorway, Annette loved watching Edie crash down the hall and back to her room. If only everyone in this dorm were like Edie, we'd all have more fun in college she thought. The distance of time and the randomness of memory left Edie perpetually rolling, rolling, rolling down that hallway, shrieking in her drunkenness, making a small detour into the "ladies" room to upchuck, to throw it all up and out, and laughing, giggling, wiping her mouth with the back of her hand, off she went into Annette's past.

Twenty years later – twenty? – how could it have been twenty years since that lovely quirky night in the dorm? Twenty years later the alumni magazine arrived in the mail, and Annette read that Edie has had five sons. Well, perfect! Nobody better prepared to handle rowdiness, loud talk, profanity, drunkenness, tardiness, the whole package, times five.

In a gust of nostalgia, Annette picked up the phone:

"I'm getting in touch with Edie. Have her over for tea. You up for it, Milt?"

And Edie came over, times without number over decades to come, laughing and late for tea every darn time, and she became a regular in Annette's quiet, buttoned-up household. Laughing. Always late. Dozens of snapshots of the "crew," as she called her five sons. Trouble was never trouble, although there was quite a bit of that. Edie always managed to make it into a long, long story with a tearfully happy ending.

"Make it a one-reeler, Edie."

*F*loating above the landscape of the living, Mrs. Zinn continued viewing, with much interest at this point, as her "whole life passed before her eyes." In this episode, it is as if Annette sits in a cool dark movie theater, in a comfortable velveteen seat that rocks slightly as the movie rises up on the enormous curving screen, and music sets the mood. Annette is in the mood for a good movie now. This was going to be a lovely afternoon matinee:

Henry Preston and Mrs. Annette Zinn sit across from each other at a table where starched pink linen napkins are folded like swans. The napkins are part of the ambiance of Bullock's Tea Room, and sunshine sweeps over the little round tables that are clad in heavily starched pink napery; sunlight picks out the beaks and wingtips of the folded swans.

The young woman who folds the napkins works in the storeroom of the Bullock's kitchen. Seated between sacks of carrots and bins of flour, she performs her deft magic. She is a part-time employee of the Bullock's Hospitality Staff. The napkin folding job is her second part-time job. Her other job is as a part-time sales clerk at the paper and art supply store that is located down the block from Bullock's. Her two jobs support, barely, her attending an art school for graduate studies. The entire map of her life as an art student is contained within a few short blocks and long cultural divides.

Her school was grubby and noisy, with ridiculous arguments about color and form and concept and echoing with the sounds of couples grappling in the store rooms. She lives nearby. She lives with another art student, a painter, and they rattle around in a very dirty, large rented retail space. He's a painter, and she is a sculptor. She is an expert at paper folding and the making of paper from scrap fibers and the Japanese artform of origami. She studied in Japan for a year, sitting at the side of a learned Japanese man who was a master of origami and paper-making.

She learned her craft as well as she could. Now she was in art school in Los Angeles. She had had the idea to make origami pieces really large. Her huge sculptures aren't made of paper, but out of wood and cardboard and some scrap metal, assembled to look like folded paper. Sort of three dimensional tromp l'oeil, she would say to anyone who asked.

Nobody asked.

Her focus as an art student involved the concepts of space and illusion and complexity and dexterity and lightness of being and making sure there was always enough toilet paper in the studio bathroom. She was happy enough, as things go. Her roommate – not her boyfriend she would insist – produced the occasional abstract painting in the style of Franz Kline. His focus was on her and on being the "next Picasso" and upon picking the seeds out of his stash and, thereafter, upon pizza or brownies or sex or all three. Oh well.

Origami was how the girl-art student got the part-time job at Bullock's Tea Room. Every morning she folded pink starched napkins into swans and bears and lions with pleated manes. The habitués of the Tea Room loved these elegant and whimsical creatures, and the "napkin-girl" was a bit of a star in this muted setting.

Sort of three dimensional tromp l'oeil, she would say to anyone who asked.

Henry Preston and Mrs. Annette Zinn come here often and usually make quite a show of looking at today's napkin creation and admiring it and making over it to the "help." Sometimes the Napkin Girl was still in the back, and once or twice they summoned her to their table so they could thank her. These were lovely and awkward moments as none of them knew how, exactly, to talk to one another. But Napkin Girl – she had a name of course, but nobody remembered it – she was gracious and shy and skittered off as quickly as possible so that she would not be considered rude by the patrons, but also so that she would not be seen by Bullock's management to be taking advantage of a situation by being overly familiar with the guests. Customers were called "guests" at the Tea Room. Never patrons. Employees were "the help." She had a name. But you never used your name if you were "the help" and the patrons – "guests" – never invited you over to their tables by calling you by your name.

Yet, somehow, Henry and Mrs. Zinn had requested to meet the Napkin Girl. And she introduced herself to them. Her name was Sarah Sax, as in saxophone. But this was a slight breach of Tea Room etiquette, and she was abruptly summoned back into the kitchen storeroom. Her "manager" reiterated the rule that "the help" was not to fraternize with the "guests." Is that clear? Yes. It was all very clear to Napkin Girl.

Mrs. Zinn plucks apart her swan napkin, fastidious, with her fingers held so as to not damage her one-hour old manicure:

"Darling. They are just darling, aren't they Henry?"

Henry picks up his napkin animal, turning it in his fingertips. It is remarkably sturdy and stiff, and he swivels it around, this way and that way, so the sunshine can rest on all the complicated little details of the folding. The napkin swan does not collapse. Then, with a sudden snap, he flaps it out to his side and places it, flattened, onto his knees.

"Oh Henry. How could you?"

Fiendish, he chuckles:

"Well, you know Mrs. Zinn, we're all going to be flattened one day. Swans and all."

"You're in a cheery mood today, Henry."

He rubs the air with his fingertips:

"Oh. You know."

They order lunch; Spring Fling Salad for Mrs. Zinn and a BLT for Henry Preston. Tea and coffee, respectively.

The food arrives. It is arranged on their plates in artful vignettes of lettuce and tomato bits and curls of this and that. Deflated, Henry looks down at his sandwich.

Mrs. Zinn just lets him be.

Just let him be, she had thought. He had days like this.

For a while, Henry worked on his sandwich and its triangles of bread and slithering tomato and shards of bacon, and when he tried to pick up one of the triangular constructions, it was just too much for him. It slipped around hopelessly and finally spilled its guts all over his plate. He fiddled with the scattered pieces, patting his lips with his wrecked swan-napkin. Gesturing to the broken sandwich, Henry said:

"You ever feel like that, Mrs. Zinn?"

"Annette. Please. Annette. A-Double-N, E-Double-T-E."

"Of course. Annette."

She picks at her salad, mining it for pieces of baby spinach or something else that, in her concentration upon Henry's mood, she had lost track of. She continues to poke, desultory, through the salad greens. Pay attention. Listen to this man. There is something wrong here today.

Henry starts up again:

"I mean. I mean. Just all flattened." He gathers his napkin to his nose and honks into it wetly.

Mrs. Zinn pauses, looking across the table at Henry, her fork hovering over her plate.

"Yes, Henry. I've had those kinds of days, too."

He sighs, a jagged breath:

"I mean, how can people be so, so *mean*, I mean."

"I know, Henry. They can."

He continues:

"I had an encounter once. It was with the very devil incarnate."

He stares down at his broken sandwich, his mouth trembling against a regurgitation of tears:

"How can people be like that, Annette?"

"How can people be like that, Annette?"

"I don't know, Henry."

At that moment Annette had not known what Henry was referring to. He got like this from time to time. As if he were on the very edge of telling her something. She sensed that, whatever it was, it had crushed him, flattened him; his words. And she knew about that kind of thing herself. Mrs. Zinn knew; she did indeed know about evil. And though, on this particular afternoon, in the Bullock's Tea Room, her intuition may not have immediately understood what Henry was referring to, she did know, intuitively, that he was re-experiencing some past injury.

She knew this. She could not have said why or how. Yet, she knew.

"Shit, Henry. Shit. I am so very sorry that you had to go through whatever it was you had to go through."

As the years progressed in Mrs. Zinn's household, Henry would discover that she was not shy of invective and that she used those sorts of words when they were most needed and only for the very worst of circumstances. At an untimely death. At an injustice. At an outrage. And hearing her say "shit" was oddly comforting, a strange balm, for the person who needed the healing. And Mrs. Zinn was what was glibly called "a good listener," but hers was a special sensitivity, a good ear she had had. And, like a musician with perfect pitch, she knew exactly when to say "shit."

She could also hear, through or around the words spoken by the mouth of her companion. Annette could hear into that person's very heart. She knew when to be silent. And she knew when to speak out.

They sit there, companionable, in this odd broken moment in the Bullock's Tea Room. Knees almost touching beneath the stiff tablecloth of their little round table. They sit there talking and taking refreshment in this gorgeous repository of perfume and silk and exquisite tailoring and suede shoes. They were almost friends at this point, mostly friends, and confidants in their way, neither of them revealing too much about themselves to the other. It was soothing seated here amongst all this luxurious paraphernalia.

Annette may have seen this movie years before. Annette

already knows this story:

You can purchase anything you want here at Bullock's. You can right every wrong here at Bullock's. Then you can sit down for a bite to eat with your parcels around your ankles. You can chat amiably, and you are surrounded by the embrace of the Tea Room, flying as far away as if you could fly to Mars. In any case, you can fly far away from annoying gravity, in the Bullock's Tea Room.

That day in the Tea Room, Mrs. Zinn had not fully understood what plunged Henry into his dark moods. Healing was only temporary. His scabs were too easily torn off and set to bleeding again. She understood now, however, savoring this memory, how our world here on earth provided only counterfeit healing by presenting us with objects of beauty, objects of no real value, but objects that we fancied would make up for anything bad that had ever happened to us.

We were only human, mused Mrs. Zinn from her new vantage point. We were only human. We were doing the best we could.

There was a pause as they each took a small bite of lunch. Henry shoved the pieces of his sandwich around on his plate:

"And this sandwich, Annette, was made by the very devil incarnate."

And they laughed a little as if it were a joke that neither of them understood. And they wiped the corners of their eyes with what was left of their napkin swans.

There are moments,
Mrs. Zinn remembers past events,
crystalline.
The tiniest details
of objects, of people, of her thoughts and of their thoughts.
Everything is revealed,
as if viewed on the surface of a still pool.
Yet,
with a subtle breeze,
the flutter of passing wings,
the slightest disturbance,
a mere tremor from beneath the watery surface,
a breath,
and it disappears.
An image may dissolve into indecipherable ripples.
Gone.
Then she loses focus.
How does this thing work?

"Henry, let's have Napkin Girl over for tea."

Henry nods, enthusiastic:

"Yes, lets."

Annette could see and hear everything as if it were only yesterday. This day with Henry and Sarah was to be so bright. Annette would lovingly remember this afternoon and mark it as a holiday – the day she and Henry and Sarah began what was to be their lifelong friendship, a joining of their hearts, and it went like this:

"And Henry – let's stop calling her Napkin Girl. Bullock's Tea Room may have their rules of engagement for "guests" and for the "help," but that's not our way. So. Tea!"

And so began a long and loving relationship created by this family of friends – Mrs. Annette Zinn, Mr. Henry Preston, and Ms. Sarah Sax. Soon enough they would simply be Annette and Henry and Sarah.

Mrs. Zinn felt the warmth and love and the sense of familiarity contained in that first moment when Napkin Girl, Sarah Sax, came to Mrs. Zinn's for tea. That was more than twenty years ago. So much was to happen.

*It is heartbreakingly
beautiful...
Words fail.
She can see and
remember this day
so clearly.
She can see and
remember how she
was on that day.*

The threesome would soon form an equilateral triangle. They would discover that they are bound by destiny. Destiny? A perfectly good word to describe these three, but Henry hated clichés, and the word "destiny" sounded so precious, too precious, to him. What had they been bound by?

On that first visit, Sarah brought a special house gift: two dozen heavily starched pink linen table napkins. She presented them to Annette in a large flat padded box that she had crafted and, for years to come, this is where the laundered and starched "flats" – as Henry came to call them – would reside. In the years to come, when the box was full of flats, Henry would summon Sarah to make her magic with them.

On that first visit, Sarah sat on the hassock in the library, chatting along as she created her first batch of origami folded napkins for Mrs. Zinn. That day she made an entire zoo. A floating swan. A lion with fanfold mane. A gazelle, running on four slender legs. An owl with feathered eyebrows. A fat bear. A zebra. A rolling kitten. A butterfly.

Folding, folding, folding and talking, talking, talking,
Sarah placed each animal on the coffee table until there was
no more room, and so she made them to march right down
the table leg and onto the floor. The whole menagerie – all
of pink linen.

It is heartbreakingly beautiful observes Mrs. Zinn as she
continues her journey toward the world to come. Words fail.
She can see and remember this day so clearly. She can see
and remember how she was on that day.

She gets down on the floor to see each folded napkin
animal right up close. And Henry does the same, tenting his
long legs up to make mountains for the little creatures.
Then, as if at a signal, they all start to rearrange the animals,
and they start to tell their stories:

"This one is the leader," says Henry.

"No, no, no. The gazelle is the leader," says Annette.

"And they are making a parade, and they all march down
the main street of a golden kingdom," says Sarah.

"A happy kingdom. No wars!"

"And everybody is happy," Sarah amends.

And the three friends make a story as they sit on the floor of the library. And the animals march and wander all across the sunbeam rug and up to Annette's chair, and Sarah makes a monkey to climb right up the chair leg.

"And I am the king of the Armchair!"

"And I, Kitty Smithers, will grab you!"

And there ensues a tussle – not to the death, but gentle, with no claws from the cat.

And they laugh and laugh and laugh; Henry and Sarah and Annette.

Aching beauty, she sees it from her vantage point at the very edge of the world to come.

Aching beauty, she sees it from her vantage point at the very edge of the world to come.

Theirs was to be the friendship of the damaged. It was a kinship of the survivor. Not that they ever talked about those kinds of things directly. They only ever made casual references to that kind of thing. And this little family of friends protected one another from each other's painful memories. There were no self-indulgent reminiscences about hurtful events. But they knew. They knew by finely tuned intuitions. Theirs was the friendship, not of secrets, but of discretion.

And, holding their folded napkin animals on their laps, patting them like live pets, they talk – all at once, all in accord:

"I just hate the current crop of misery memoirs."

"Yeah, me too. It's a contest to see who has had the most horrible life."

"Victims."

"Deaths."

"Dismemberments."

They laugh. They are in lively accord – Annette and Henry and Sarah. This fad for literary confessionals – the more grotesque, the better it seemed – the three friends agreed: they couldn't stand those things. Their attitude could have been called "denial." But, more accurately, Sarah and Henry and Annette preferred to elide their own pain, at least in conversation. There were no excruciating confessionals when they got together.

"I was born immediately after the atomic bombs were dropped," said Sarah.

Theirs was the friendship, not of secrets, but of discretion.

Annette listens, hesitating with her response:

"And the camps were discovered. By soldiers. Those soldiers set free the skeletal souls who had survived. Those souls were still clinging to those bones, barely clinging to life itself."

"Those photographs." Henry drifts off.

"Yes. And that is all I have ever seen. Photographs," said Annette.

Annette was only a minor survivor in the population of survivors. She had survived her mother's death. But she had been born in a place where her survival would not be particularly remarkable. She was born in the United States where, even at the height, or depths, of the world at war, it was a place where no bombs were dropped. Living through that period of time was not heroic survival but simply sheer good luck. Tu, tu, tu; do not tempt the devil. Annette's survival had not been tested by war. And she may not have felt *whole* after her mother's death, but she had, indeed, had her whole life ahead of her.

Sarah strokes her napkin gazelle. Annette brings her

pink swan right up to her face, beak to nose and makes a voice for it, tipping the little bird back and forth as she speaks for it:

"There, but for fortune, go I."

Henry makes his monkey to put its hands to its face. See no evil.

Sarah brings Kitty Smithers up, clasping her tightly to her heart.

Annette makes her napkin swan to swim, rocking it back and forth along the beam of sunlight that edges slowly along the carpet, in the library, in the late afternoon, after tea at Mrs. Zinn's.

ow that Mrs. Zinn is headed for "the world to come," she can visit her own distant past selves. Times past – with her mother or with her husband or with friends or even with strangers who could pop up unexpectedly. And, whether or not she chose which of her past lives, so to speak, she could see them all, as each one popped up. She could see them, very clearly. In fact, she could see those past events of her life with minute clarity. She had more clarity now than she had been able to muster during her actual experiences of certain events.

Now she sees herself at fifteen.

Such a young fifteen she had been. Not worldly, nor wise. On today's standard of sophistication, she would have been declared "retarded" – although she fully understood how that word had been retired from everyday usage. Still, that was the state of Mrs. Zinn's intelligence about the world when she was fifteen.

Annette Zinn, at fifteen, lived in the world of literature and fiction, of stories, and often she misunderstood those stories, misinterpreted them entirely. Alexander Dumas'

Camille was her current favorite. So romantic! She could not, at fifteen, discern the sorrows of that abused heroine, the darkness of the passions in the heroine's life – a "call-girl" she would have been labeled in today's jargon. Or worse. The young Annette was transfixed by her own teenage notions, and she saw this story as beautiful and tragic and transcendent.

Entering her favorite bookstore of that era, Mrs. Zinn could see and feel all of those silly-girl feelings again as she was about to experience real betrayal, real abuse, and to escape from real danger for the first time in her life. Her teenaged self flooded back to her the moment she heard the tinkle of the little bell that was perched on the top of the door to the shop.

This, her first grown-up job, working in that bookstore. Oh, treasured foolish aspiration. Bobbing at the ceiling of the bookstore, Mrs. Zinn watches it all unfold:

Annette is shelving books. Paperbacks with their evocative scent of ink and paper and magical worlds to devour. She is so happy in her menial role in that little bookstore.

The owner seems pleased with her work. He watches her as she scrabbles on her knees, stocking the lower shelves.

She stands up, a bit breathless from her efforts.

He, a man with thick white hair, maybe sixty or, if prematurely white-haired, he might have been only forty.

He walks up to her.

He stands still in front of her.

He does not speak.

He reaches out with both his hands.

He cups his hands around her jaws.

He gently – it will be recorded – takes her chin, gently, into his hands.

He moves forward to kiss her on the lips.

From her place in the world to come, Mrs. Zinn looks on.

Oh, poor little thing.

Poor me.

In a few years, this kind of entitled male aggression will be scandalously immortalized in literature. But for now, for the time being, this bookstore owner is no more than a sordid distant cousin, a libidinous ancestor, of the character

In a few years,
this kind of entitled
male aggression will be
scandalously
immortalized in
literature.

who would emerge from that infamous book. On that day, in that bookstore, when Annette was just fifteen, this man was just a dog-eared, marked-down Humbert Humbert.

And that was that.

Annette had managed to get away somehow. Her guardian angel stepping between them. Or maybe it was simply quitting time. She escaped, yes. But never forgot.

"Fuck you, you fucking fucker," she said hovering from her vantage point in the world to come.

She liked the freedom of today's invective. She had never been shy of using it. Too bad she could not have used it then, when the white hair and the hands and those lips drew near to her little fifteen-year-old self. At fifteen, she had barely even known of the word "fuck". She saw it one time, knifed into the wood of a railroad tie. With a shiver, she had intuited it's meaning, even back then.

If only.

If only she had been able to talk with Henry and Sarah about that bookstore owner. But, of course, that would never do. You don't talk about things like that. You do not taint a friendship with loose talk and confessionals.

Somehow little Annette had weaseled out of the man's grasp. And somehow, she had managed to weasel out of this, her first grown-up job.

What she told her mother was a series of obfuscations, not the truth. Never. Her mother, maybe wise enough to see through to the truth or maybe just too preoccupied to notice, her mother asked her:

"Was anybody in the store with you today?"

"No, Mama."

Then nobody saw it. It did not happen. Then her mother said:

"Let's go over to Bullock's and find that little tennis bracelet you've been wanting. And, while we're there, let's get a bite to eat at the Tea Room."

And, regardless of whether her mother was wise or simply expedient, she gave Annette the script: tell on him, and you will be destroyed. Keep it to yourself, and we'll go shopping.

Fuck the fucking fucker.

his is not rocket science; roulette. Yet mathematical minds, some quite gifted in math and science, have wasted valuable mental resources and fleeting hours of their lives calculating more favorable mathematical odds for what is, in the final analysis, a fools' game. No matter how you slice it, it's for chumps. The odds are always, always, with the house. Roulette.

You would think it would be quicker to simply throw your money into the river. Or, here's an idea: hand that wad of cash to that homeless person over there.

Annette remembers, and now she receives images, from a long-forgotten incident in her past. And, more than just images, she can perceive subtleties in events that she had missed when they had actually taken place.

At twenty-one I was old enough to stand by my father's side in the casinos, as he placed his bets. A girl-croupier calls out, sexy dominatrix:

"Rein ne va plus."

I saw that my father was flushed and that he breathed a bit rough and his glance, back and forth, between the mesmerizing click and spin of the wheel and the girl-croupier's cleavage and the metal ball skips in rhythmic rat-tat-tatter-tat in its race in the opposite direction of the spin. I saw that he was getting off on this little game. He was teetering on explosion as the tension rose. He could win. He could win. He might win. Biting his tongue: he might win. He will win.

He lost.

Then Annette sees, as if in a dream:

"La Croupier is wearing my dress. It is my prom dress, fancy and lowcut."

Mrs. Zinn calls out:

"Hey! That's my . . ."

But from her place in the world to come, she cannot intercede. Yet, she finally realizes – all these decades later – what actually took place down there.

It was her prom dress the croupier was wearing. The little dress she bought for her first big party. Pink chiffon drifting over rose sateen. A cloud. It was her prom dress that she had left in her old closet in her parents' home after she had married Milton. The girl-croupier was wearing her dress.

It was her father's idea? Was it his fetish?

By then she knew the rules. She knew how the game is played. She gets into her car, swings away from the casino, fast, and onto the street. A trash can teeters.

"Well, well, Dad. What's with you and your little prom queen?"

Annette did not say those words to him at that point. But a long-forgotten memory, perhaps from one of her rabbi's classes that she had attended, comes to mind: what she remembers now from her new vantage point is something about: "*. . . leave your father's house . . .*" She had, back then, done just that.

"And it was my prom dress. That's creepy."

Well. Well.

"You are dead to me now."

The scene changes now. Annette is married to Milton. Kind and lovely Milton. Milt. Milton, secular and despite all that, it was Milton who purchased the mezuzah for

their first home. She had teased him, back about a million years ago:

"But Milton. You never do anything Jewish."

But now that he had purchased and installed their first mezuzah, she dubbed him ever afterwards, "Milton of the Mezuzah."

Annette well remembers her dad arranging to meet Milton for lunch in a nice fancy restaurant, just the two of them. Annette is happy that they want to get acquainted. Milton comes home. Girlish and anxious to hear about how her two men got along, she asks:

"How did it go, Milt?"

Milton shakes his head. Not in the negative, but in a manner that looks like incredulity.

"Your father started to talk up the waitress. When she leaves our table, he turns to me, sort of chummy, man-to-man, and he's talking trash about what he'd like to do to, or with her, our waitress."

Annette, bobbing up by her ceiling, suddenly gets it. Repulsed, she watches.

"Is that okay, Milt?"

Milton puts his arm around her shoulders:

"No, Annette. It is not okay."

Then she sees her prom dress on the girl-croupier. Her dress. From her bird's eye view of her life from the world to come, she takes it all in. All of it. She knows this game. It's a chump's game. The odds are always with the house.

Nobody had seen what Annette had seen. Nobody would ever step up to affirm her memories.

"Okay. Okay. Okay. I get it. I get it. But don't you forget; I never forgot.

"Les jeux sont faits, Papa."

istening and talking, we learn about one another. The Napkin Girl and I visit as often as we can over the years. Of course, she is Sarah Sax, now.

My mother died when I was twenty-two. Sarah's mother also died when Sarah was twenty-two.

We discover that she and I belong to that club. That club nobody wants to join. But there we were. Daughters without mothers. There's nothing else like it for producing crazy-haired women, stubborn women, women who shed unexpected tears behind their tinted glasses at unexpected moments of recollection that could strike anywhere, anytime. Tears could roll out at a stoplight on the corner of Wilshire and Little Santa Monica, for example. Right there, right then, would flow unexpected tears. Sarah and I were members in that club. Nobody could have understood. But we both knew, instantly, what was meant by our being daughters without mothers.

There are certain bonds, ephemeral, that bind the orphaned. Oh, and let's not be too dramatic, the partially-orphaned. The motherless girl-child.

Some dads, widowed, go on and make new lives. They shrug off the hard parts of dealing with those needy daughters. How dare those girls dramatize their pain? What pains these lonesome girls become! Why can't they just get a grip?

There is a wedding.

It is held at the family residence where Annette had lived with her parents.

There is a wedding. It's in the big house, Annette's former family home, on Angelus Mundi Drive. What kind of name is that for a street?

There were no seats in the front row of the event. No little name card spelled out the name "Annette."

Annette wanders through the room at her parents' house. Former. She wanders among the guests, the witnesses-to-be as her father re-marries in her former family home – her own mother's house. All the adorable little white folding chairs are occupied by strangers. What's that line about "...*leave your father's house?*"

Annette moves to the back of the room, taking a spot,

standing room only, next to a neighbor, Mrs. Stern, a neighbor and a former close friend of Annette's mother.

The solemn words are spoken. And that is that. That's it. Done. During the middle passage, Mrs. Stern slips her arm around Annette's waist and hugs her, firmly, and keeps her upright. And for those hollow moments, Annette is cherished and supported by this near-stranger, her dead mother's friend.

May her memory be for a blessing.

Mrs. Zinn wonders:

Is, was, this now, or then?
Am I, or was I, here, or there, then or now?
Was that then, or is this now?
Was that me, or is this me, now?
Where am, or was, I?
Is this now, or then, or when?
If not now, when?
I am, or was, so confused.
Am I here?
Or there?
Or where?
Is this now?
Or then?
Did this happen?
Or is this happening?
How can I see without having seen?
How now?
But not then?
I am so confused.
Was I always so confused?
Will I be thus, further, confused?
Where am I?
Here or there?
Or nowhere?
Am I lost?
Forgotten?
Both?
Neither?

And now, she slides gratefully into the memories of her husband, Milton. What a relief to see Milton again. Annette hears his voice as he provides the narration to a series of glimpses into their life together. Milton remembers when they met:

"Remember, Annette? Remember when we met? You wore that striped skirt – its stripes lined up like chevrons."

"You had sad eyes, Milt."

"You swept me off my feet."

"We were dancing. Feet were involved, Milty."

Then there is the bedroom scene:

Flannel-sheet nights were the best and embraced them during their earliest sleeps. There were the usual things. The thumb that hooks the pale blue bikini elastic, sliding the little garment all the way down her slender thighs. You know. All the usual things. Then mornings:

"Let's have the croissants in bed, Milty."

And the buttery flakes float and then nestle, itchy, into the delicious, buttery flannel sheets. There is a little crunchy sound as we turn to taste on our lips each other's coffee and

Paris rolls and raspberry jam.

Almost better is the talk. Tangled up in flannel, we lie there, knees folded up and bumping and:

"Remember school playgrounds?"

"Yes. And sitting in a sliver of shade, right on the hot tar, and it smelled like hot tar."

Milton grins:

"What a coincidence."

"Don't make fun, Milt. Sitting on the hot tar, I discovered I could make tar balls by scraping the heels of my Buster Browns along, and I could roll up tar balls. I made a bunch of them, lined them up next to my skirt, before I got caught."

"You're in TROUBLE, Nettie!"

"Oh yes. My mother and the principal demanded to know what on earth I thought I was doing, making tar balls."

Turning, muffled, in our flannel sheets, onto our backs:

"It was an experiment, Mama."

In sickness and in health. Of course, when you are

twenty-five and a little nervous standing there being married, it's not hard at all to pledge this. It's just words. It's just tradition. Just repeat after me. Just say it.

Then, later, much later, there was intense pain. Annette was sick for a while. Mostly the attacks were at night. Nausea and vomiting and slow, rhythmic clenching pains, like what she thought labor would feel like. Labor, in pulsing cramping pains, closer and closer in timing, like labor pains. But no joyous wails of the infant at the end of the seizures. None of that for Annette. And she would lie on her back between bouts, and Milton brings the flannel top sheet over to comfort her, and he is anxious; will she die? And Annette loved that warm flannel, and she would have loved it more if another round of cramping labor were not already starting; this labor without the prize, without the infant, born and wailing and healthy. She had told her doctors about the attacks; the intensity of the pains, and they had only tut-tutted:

"Buck up, little girl."

Then, finally, the reprieve. And her surgeon, with her

clipboard, says to her:

"You could have died, Annette."

Punitive, the surgeon admonished her:

"You should have told us."

I did. I did. I did.

But Annette never said that to her surgeon.

She went home to the flannel envelope and, even though her body was no longer *whole*, she still had her whole life ahead of her and, released from pain, she could now be wholly and more fully present with Milton.

"You did a big bar mitzvah party, Milt?"

"No. Not big."

"How come? Didn't your parents want to put on a big DO?"

"It was my project, Annette."

"What do you mean?"

"For my bar mitzvah project, I proposed to give away all the money we would have spent on a big party to homeless people in our city."

Annette turns onto her side, folding her elbow with her

hand to support her head.

"But instead of just handouts, I told the rabbi and my father that I wanted to engage each homeless person in real conversation. Not just me yak, yak, yakking at them. But me, listening, and writing down their stories. You know. It would be my bar mitzvah project."

No. Annette did not know. Girls did not do bar mitzvahs back then. I guess it's called bat mitzvah now. Now girls do them.

"I told the rabbi I wanted to make a genizah in our synagogue."

The rabbi, unaccustomed to being told much of anything constructive from such a young boy, asked Milt:

"Where did you learn about genizahs, Milty?"

"I read about them in the encyclopedia, Rabbi."

Rabbi sits there unblinking:

"And what will go into this genizah, Milt?"

"Well, sir, old scrolls and pieces of paper that have the word God on them and, and the stories I will write down about the lives of the homeless people that I give money to."

The boy shows unusual clarity for his age. He understands Torah completely.

"And these stories of the homeless – how do you know that they will include the word God in them?"

"Well, Rabbi, theirs are God-given lives, so in that way the word God will be an intrinsic part of their stories."

Oy.

The boy shows unusual clarity for his age. He understands Torah completely.

"And where would we put our synagogue's genizah, Milton?'

"In the store room, Rabbi."

"With all the brooms and mops and buckets?"

"Well, Rabbi, those objects represent acts of loving-kindness to our members. And that's to sanctify God too, right, Rabbi?"

You cannot argue with this. The rabbi glances over at Milton's father. Milton's father is suppressing a tiny smile and staring, fascinated, by something on the rabbi's study ceiling.

"And so, that was my project, Annette."

She snuggles over to him and whispers:

"Milton Mordechai Zinn."

And Milton was bar mitzvah and there was no big fancy party.

Who shall live and who shall die? And when? Not now. Not yet. Please.

Embracing under their flannel sheets, Annette slides her hands up Milton's back.

Later, pulling the laundry from the hot dryer, Annette finds Milton's blue cotton boxers tangled up in the flannel sheets. She folds them neatly and puts them on top of the pile.

So many billions of us.
Each and every one thinks we're one-of-a-kind.
Isn't that preposterous?
How preposterous for any one of us to think
that our particular wishes will be granted as we beseech
the heavens above.
How dare we believe that our little needs will be met
with the full and loving attention of God?
Whoever he, she, or it may be?
It is beyond comprehension.
We are so entirely self-absorbed
that some of us even believe that we can
ask and then receive grace.

Mary E. Carter

"We have company."

It's as if Henry were right here, right now. He is speaking through the closed door to Mrs. Zinn's bedroom suite:

"They're here. It's the people from the "Y." A man and a woman. They both have clipboards."

"Okay, Henry. I'll be down in ten minutes. You go ahead and start. Take them into the dining room and serve them the tea and the snacks we decided on."

Henry had already set the table for a nice afternoon tea party. Pretty china – not the very best china, but charming in its way. Henry was an expert at what he called turning teacups. He loved plunking around in odd consignment shops, picking up a cup here, a dish there, and always looking on the bottom first to determine its lineage, then to consider its maker, and then to, perhaps, make up a fantasy history of the piece. Annette had watched him doing this, countless times, observing him across a room filled with chairs and lamps and piles of old crockery and china. He had a certain look, fussy, critical, as he went about his

She had a very impressive firm handshake.

exploration, giving every dish in the place a discerning little peek. If a cup did not pass muster, he'd gently put it down, shake his head, and sigh.

Today Henry had laid out cookies, mixed nuts, and little triangle sandwiches with a light whipped cheese and shreds of cucumber embedded, firmly, into the mixture. Henry despised tea sandwiches that fell apart, and over the years he'd invented several ways to avoid sandwich disasters. He had also provided iced water in crystal glasses. Then he spent several happy moments moving the pink folded swan napkins this way and that. Today he positioned them as if they were floating from place setting to place setting. The effect was more fun if there were eight or more diners, but it wasn't bad with just the four of them this afternoon.

Mrs. Zinn joined the tea drinkers with her serious face. A short woman, she could still command a room with an expression of interested curiosity, but her jutting chin provided a contrast, a challenge. She strode up to them. To their very great credit, they both shot up from their seats to shake her extended hand. She had a very impressive, firm handshake. Milton, may his memory be a blessing, had taught her that handshake. He told her that when she took over the foundation, when he died, that she would need to assume a businesslike demeanor. She should be smiling, but never chummy. Listen carefully to these fund-raising presentations. Watch out for liars and cheats. Never do business on a Monday. Be direct. Do not equivocate. Speak up. Go by your gut. And it would all work out. She was good at it. Milton discovered Annette had the best bullshit detector on the planet — at least on this particular planet. He was proud of her and told her so:

"There might be no accounting for bullshit in the world to come, my dear. But for this world, you are in great shape."

She took her place at the head of the table.

There was a presentation. PowerPoint. Graphs. Projections. Pictures of events at the "Y" — kids swimming, handicrafts classes, people in the auditorium. Then last, but not least, the dramatic conclusion — a photograph of an aging, somewhat dingy van. More information — it seated

Milton discovered Annette had the best bullshit detector on the planet.

The Lodz Ghetto Photographs of Henryk Ross

eight adults or twelve children. It got 20 miles per gallon of gasoline. It was a Dodge, no longer a vintage model. And the point? They were fund-raising for its replacement.

Mrs. Zinn asked:

"How much is a new van?"

"Twenty thousand dollars."

Annette and Henry glance across the teacups. Henry clears his throat.

Mrs. Zinn asks:

"It would be exclusively for the use of the "Y"?

"Yes, Mrs. Zinn. In fact, the YMCA logo and some other decorative body painting would be added to a new white van after it is purchased."

"Would you excuse me for a moment. Mr. Preston will refresh your tea. I will be right back."

She went upstairs to her little desk. Beside it were bookshelves with many volumes. She took a battered, oversized picture book down and leafed through the photographs, turning a few of its well-worn pages. Pages that she knew almost by heart.

There. There. And then.

There, but for fortune, go I, she thought. Never forget, she thought.

And with these images, these ghosts, seared into her mind at this moment, she wrote the check, the only check that the fund-raisers from the "Y" would need for the purchase of a whole new van.

"Milton?"

She knew that he was there with her now. And she knew that he understood what she was doing. And they agreed, that, yes, this was the right thing to do.

I have been enabled to do this. I am enabled by my circumstances. I might have been born as any child, in any land, during any era, facing any catastrophe, experiencing any horror. Yet, here I am, and I have been here for my entire life. And I am enabled to do this.

And, floating now, gently bobbing against her own ceiling, Annette remembers – not because she truly does remember, but perhaps she is being nudged by someone who reminds her of this quote from Pirke Avot:

There, but for fortune, go I, she thought. Never forget, she thought.

"*It is not up to you to finish the work, yet you are not free to avoid it.*"

And, in fact, Annette responds:

"I was born here, now, in this place. I am free to do whatever I will. And so, freely, I take on this work."

Another fund-raising committee comes for tea. It's an event Annette remembers from a very long time ago. Milton was still alive, and Henry Preston was not yet a member of her household. This was a big one. This fund-raiser has stood out in Annette's memories – she has never forgotten its importance, its disturbances, in her adult life. This is not easy. Why do I need to rehash these things, she wonders? Why now? It's not as if I can do anything to change any of it.

Today it is the Downtown Homeless Women's Shelter. Two representatives come armed with clipboards and brochures. This is long before the era of PowerPoint presentations. They have a slide show – sunny dining room and women are smiling in conversation or looking directly at the camera with beaming smiles. The missing tooth, the cracked lips put the lie to these cheerful snapshots. Annette knows. These are pictures to assuage the guilt and to convince the donors that they may be absolved from that feeling of guilt, or even for feeling a trace of uneasiness, as they pen their names onto the symbols of their personal

Why do I need to rehash these things, she wonders? Why now?

generosity: their checks. See. These homeless women are okay, happy, even.

Annette knows better. She has always known:

"There, but for fortune, go I."

And she could see it clearly now; she could sense the truth of these women:

In a clean, spare, delivery room, three attendants see to a patient who is giving birth. They have fastened large aprons, haphazard, over their pink scrubs. They are working hard to usher in this new life. Their surgical masks are stained with sweat, and they give terse, muffled instructions to the little girl on the table. For it is a little girl. Who made her pregnant? There are the usual blood and screams, and she is twelve, maybe. The attendants communicate to the girl with equal parts of piety and of cruelty. She, this girl, will surely go to hell. But nobody actually says this to her. Yet they do inform her that this pain is in payment for all fun she must have had that ultimately landed her in this predicament. It's hopeless. Without hope. This little mother is beyond redemption, and that is evident in the brusque orders from

the women around the table. God will deal with her. But
meanwhile, she must be shamed. She deserves it. She's a
wayward girl. She's in trouble. An unwed mother. There are
so many names for what she has become: ruined, fallen,
damaged goods, slut, floozy, whore, nymphomaniac. And
the Thesaurus lists a single given name for this little girl and
the entry says: "Jezebel, noun, prostitute."

The girl whimpers between contractions:

"Hey, he's unwed too. What about him?"

At worst, he may be called a womanizer. But he may also
be called, with a wink and a nudge, a real charmer, ladies'
man, playboy, rake, stud, wolf. And there are several given
names for this lad, too, names that come from literature,
from opera, from Shakespeare even: Casanova, Romeo, Don
Juan, Rhett Butler. Romantic, dashing, heroes even. Sought
after by little girls who feel empowered by falling for the
"rebel without a cause." So romantic.

Never mind. He will marry well. You? You this girl,
victim of your own bad behavior: ruined, tainted. You are
forever labeled by your night in the sack. Or, more likely, on

*Casanova, Romeo,
Don Juan, Rhett Butler.
Romantic, dashing,
heroes even. Sought
after by little girls who
feel empowered by
falling for the
"rebel without a cause."
So romantic.*

the backseat of that Chevy out on Mulholland Drive.

But it was so romantic.

The women who work to deliver unwanted infants disperse good works and harsh judgment. They whisk the bundles, newborns – this one is a girl-child – striding, righteous, down an immaculate linoleum hallway. One of these women will "place" – it is called "placing" – she will place this infant into the arms of a waiting "mother." The hopeful "mother." This stranger, now a mother, will not smell like this infant's birth-mother. This girl-infant will never, ever, smell her own mother again. It is a wound that will reside in this infant's deepest precognitive depths. This wound, a separation wound, is a gash that may never be forgotten. This separation wound is not easily shaken off, neither by the infant nor by its birth mother. And, ironically, this wound will never even be remembered, in the first place, by this infant, this girl-child who is placed into the arms of a stranger.

Yet this rupture will be recorded. It will reside within the hidden memory of this little being who is placed in the very first seconds of her life, into the arms of a mother who is not her mother. It defies reason. It defies humanity. Ordinary kindness, it defies. It defies the odds that this infant can live a so-called normal life. These nascent memories, of simultaneous birth followed by immediate abandonment, may put in place a muscle-memory of cruel abuse that could program this child into a less than solid future. There can reside, in the constitution of this child, anxiety and a fight-or-flight reflex that might influence her adult responses as her life develops.

Oh, sure. There are the happy exceptions. There are happy adoptions. It can assuage guilt for us to think so. But Annette had observed, throughout her lifetime, that orphans conceived and born of these harsh and earliest moments of rough handling cannot ever, completely, recover.

Words fail.

Annette perceives that such an infant may replicate, by some sad soul's reckoning, being an orphan forever. Having been removed from its first home, from her birth-mother, this infant is born with a predestined burden.

The subconscious instruction might predestine such an infant to live, forever, without a home. This kind of predestined message may be fiendishly hard to overcome. Granted, again, it may be said that some babies with this imprint will be able to overrule the pattern of the embodied instructions. But overcoming the notion of being a homeless orphan may prove to be almost impossible to achieve for some girl-child babies and their birth-mothers.

Let's say the baby is placed in a loving home. There will be many snapshots documenting her happy life, in her happy new home, with her orphan-mother.

Later, when she is mostly grown up, the hidden pain of her early separation and abandonment may be simply too much for her to overcome. Then there may follow the unfolding of her struggles to resist her early conditioning.

Later still, one of her family snapshots might be reluctantly handed to the police officer whose duty it is to tend and to monitor the homeless in his city. He keeps a file on these homeless women. They are photographed again and again as they age, year by year, on the streets, and as they are arrested, again and again, for polluting these golden and indifferent streets. These streets are in a city that houses millionaires and billionaires in their sky-high condominiums, high above the sick and dirty humps of the homeless women who sleep down there on the steaming grates of the sidewalks. Those homeless women are neighbors to unimaginable wealth and to feckless indifference.

A homeless woman is routinely chipped, like a dog.

This is so that she may be identified when she is found, murdered, while sleeping under a bush, on the grounds of a nearby fast food restaurant. Police gather up the contents of her meagre bundle, which have been scattered on the parking lot. Maybe it was drug related. Who knows? Who cares?

Now, for this fundraising pitch, Mrs. Zinn is shown the cheerful pictures of the homeless women who dine in the Downtown Homeless Women's Shelter. These smiling photographs are a desecration, in a sense, of the precious and hidden lives of these women's souls, still and ever after, orphans in the streets.

There are,
in your care,
the hearts
of these women.

Annette interrupts the presentation.

"We will help you fund all operational expenses. And Mr. Zinn and I will also provide a provision in our trust to continue funding operational expenses, even after our deaths. We want also to serve on your board of directors. It's time for our personal involvement. If not now, when? With all due respect, our financial support can only help you so much with this shelter. Above and beyond management concerns, rules and regulations and such, there are, in your care, the hearts of these women. Damaged women. Each with her story. Some of it may be unbearable. But the task is as much to mend hearts as it is to finance the institution. And so, this is what we propose: if you can accept our offer of support above and beyond mere dollars, if you would be willing to let us help to mend these broken women, we would be honored to serve on your board."

Milton understood, very clearly, how and why Annette had seemingly, and so quickly, made this decision. It was not, actually, a quick decision. It was something more rooted for her. Milton knew this about Annette: he knew

that even though she would protest that she was wholly
secular and that she had not paid attention to the many
classes she had taken over her lifetime, nevertheless, she had
good instincts, regardless of where or how she got them, and
she knew, very well that:

*"It is not up to you to finish the work, yet you are not
free to avoid it."*

Now, however, from her new perspective – on her way
into the world to come – as an observer of her own past life,
of her own past intentions, both hidden and forgotten, she
could discern that she may have had what her mother used
to call "notions" about those homeless women and how to
help them. And, sadly, Annette realizes that she might have
been wrong. Her intuition at the time, about the souls of
those homeless women and what they needed, may have
been just plain wrong.

What if she had been wrong?

She had believed that the combination of her financial
support, along with her voluntary participation on the
board of directors, would do some good in the end. The end

result was good. Wasn't it? Her hope had been to reduce the numbers of homeless women. To find them, if not homes, at the very least, shelter.

But nothing had changed in the world of those homeless women. In fact, on the day that Mrs. Zinn found herself floating above, and separated from, her life on this earth, the homeless women's population was even greater than it had been when she took on the task to help those women, many decades ago.

As the decades had passed since Mrs. Zinn had begun to help and to support care for homeless women, their world had gotten worse, not better. Homeless women may have experienced one or all of many horrors: domestic violence, childhood sexual abuse, adult partner abuse, cultural devaluation of women, gender hierarchical power-plays. They might have been battered, stalked, or harassed. Homeless women were poor, on the leading edge of the decline of federal or state assistance. Homeless women received few if any benefits from employment, including low wages, few affordable employer insurance options and, rarely, any child care. Women often receive harsher punishments for similar crimes that men commit. Most homeless women have been, at one time or another, involved in prostitution, drug dealing, shoplifting, and incarceration "for their own good." They experience sexual victimization, physical victimization, and victimization by authorities, including those in law enforcement. Homeless women suffer from lack of health care, including cancer screening, prenatal care, ambulatory care, and specialty care. They face hypertension, arthritis, mental illness, substance abuse, STIs such as chlamydia, herpes, genital warts, gonorrhea, syphilis, or trichomonas, not to mention tuberculosis and HIV. And, as if all this were not bad enough, they will suffer lack of basic care during menstruation: lack of clean changing areas and little or no access to fresh tampons, pads, or privacy. If their mental health deteriorates, is it any wonder that they suffer further with antisocial personality behaviors, depression, stress, and post-traumatic stress disorder?

Their world is a horrible place.

The broken world was still, and forevermore would be, subjected to shattering.

Yet, surely Mrs. Zinn had done some good, had helped women in this world?

Now, however, from this vantage point, she could see and understand flaws in her thinking. That she could overcome human adversity and the venality of the world, was this not hubris on her part? Her own personal form of hubris? Was this not oversimplification of the extent to which she, Mrs. Annette Zinn, could act upon the world to make it better? And let's not be coy: that she could use her money to mend the broken world?

This is the conundrum of tikkun olam. She could see that now.

This was hard. The broken world was still, and forevermore would be, subjected to shattering. Even as we tried to mend it, it was smashing all around our heads.

Having this insight was painful. Maybe she had not lived the life she had thought she had. Had she been overconfident in her powers to make the world a better place for the homeless women? Well, she thinks: We were doing the best we could. We were only human.

From Google:

"**Broken heart syndrome**. *This condition —
often brought on by stressful situations that can
cause severe, but usually temporary, heart muscle failure —
occurs more commonly in women after menopause. This
condition may also be called takotsubo cardiomyopathy,
apical ballooning syndrome, or stress cardiomyopathy.*

"**Takotsubo cardiomyopathy**, *also known as* **stress
cardiomyopathy**, *is a type of non-ischemic cardiomyopathy
in which there is a sudden temporary weakening of the
muscular portion of the heart. This weakening may be
triggered by emotional stress, such as the death of a loved
one, a break-up, rejection from a partner or constant
anxiety.*"

The heart breaks. Not just a metaphor. This is a genuine
medical condition. Stress cardiomyopathy. Google said so,
right?

Once a heart is broken, the possessor of that heart can
perceive broken hearts all around her.

This. This is the conundrum of tikkun olam.

*Once a heart
is broken, the possessor
of that heart can
perceive broken hearts
all around her. This.
This is the conundrum
of tikkun olam.*

Mrs. Zinn could see that now. This was hard. The broken world was still, and would be forevermore, shattering. Even as she had tried to mend it, the world was breaking. When one heart breaks, it breaks again and again, especially when witnessing other hearts breaking. Simply living this life, every heart is broken sooner or later. Probably. Right?

This is real.

*B*ut there is more.

"Oh, foolish and blind woman! How could I have been so blind?"

Her realization is physically manifested. She starts bobbing around overhead, quite violently. She is like a bundle of helium balloons on a windy afternoon.

With a rush of intuition, Mrs. Zinn finally "gets it." If only she had had access to these things, forgotten or hidden. If only she had seen these things during her life.

The conundrum of tikkun olam is not simply to do good works to mend a broken world. The conundrum of tikkun olam is how, and why, we choose certain parts to fix. Why fix broken women rather than, say, fixing the opera? Or fixing an old hospital? Or fixing forests? Or fixing schools? Or – name any other broken thing in this world's sorrowful broken state – why do we select one thing over another for our own personal tikkun olam?

Mrs. Zinn realizes now, too late of course: "My own heart had been broken. There. I have said it. Of course."

Well. Well.

I had been like those women: grieving, broken, subjected to gender power-plays, and left to fend for myself, broken-hearted. Had I simply forgotten or ignored my own experiences? Apparently, my own feelings were hidden from my own consciousness until now, until this very end of my own existence. Now it's too late to do anything. Why now?

"Now, vividly, the experiences of the homeless women, worlds removed from my own comfortable world, simply made my blood boil. All those broken hearts."

What is it about sky that makes us think of Heaven, capital H, she wonders?
Why couldn't heaven be found in dirt?
The dirt of a garden, for example?
In dirt there are a million microscopic and very lively creatures,
pushing through the pebbles,
crunching them into compost,
making the dirt into food.
Or what if heaven were like a picture sent from lightyears away from
the Hubble Space Telescope?
We are so small.
Really, we are quite unmeasurably tiny.
And so presumptuous.
How come we believe that the sky is home to heaven?
Ridiculous creatures that we are.
Oh well.
We were only human.
We were doing the best we could.

PLEASE DO NOT ENTER WITHOUT KNOCKING. PLEASE DO NOT KNOCK.

—JACK LONDON

Mrs. Zinn craved solitude. She needed time to replenish her energy, especially after the fundraising meetings. Part of her was emptied out by all her duties.

And, now, even at this moment of life review, Annette needed a rest. Perhaps she had not been who or what she had thought she was. It was too much. And, certainly now, there was nothing she could do about, any of it, anyway.

Please let me catch my breath, she thought. And, as if her thought was an order for whoever was directing this newsreel, she found a moment of quiet in her life review:

In her calendar, there were days marked with an "S" for solitude. That meant a day without visitors, without doctor appointments, without company, except for their own company – Annette Zinn and Henry Preston.

She and Henry would burrow under, as they called it, both of them engaged in silent activities. He would patter here and there around the place, perhaps snipping off dried leaves from the potted roses while Annette strolled through her little domain. She would straighten a small framed oil

painting here. Or she would peek into her own desk drawers there. Sometimes she felt like a spy, right in her own home.

She would rediscover the drawer in her desk where she stored blank books. She had dozens of these little books – leather-bound or covered in padded silk. Some of the blank books were bound in entire reproductions of famous paintings – front, spine, and back covers that had a continuous view of a single painting. So many small notebooks.

She supposed that they were to be used for poems, or for diary entries, or even for datebooks. She opened several that particular morning of solitude. Where had all these little books come from?

Annette thought back and remembered that some of the books had been brought to her as gifts. She also remembered going to the nearby stationery store when she wanted to get someone a baby gift or a bar mitzvah pen, and she would stop to look at the rack that held the blank books and, often, she would purchase another blank book along with her gift. And she would come home, and Henry would wrap the gift, and she would put her latest blank book into her desk drawer, along with all the others.

During a certain kind of day, in solitude and perhaps when she was feeling nostalgic, she'd pick through her assortment of blank books and search for some mark or a word that she might have jotted down. Nothing. There was not one thing. Not a word or numeral. All of her blank books were blank.

Day Three

The old sofa embraced us.
We snuggled into our flannel nightgowns,
drinking hot cocoa.
What to make of that day?
What questions could we have asked?
Candle Unburn.

Mary E. Carter

Now it is a rainy day at Sarah's house. How clearly Annette remembers it. She can see it now, reenacted, as if it were happening right now. She can feel her own emotions, and Sarah's, as she and Sarah sat talking.

Sarah is sitting, legs folded, scrunched deep into the somewhat shabby pillows of her old gray sofa. It's not that Sarah could not afford a new sofa to replace her old sofa. She simply could not bear to part with the poor old thing; it was now a warm, embracing living creature. That old sofa had been with her throughout her whole adult life. Sarah was about thirty-five at that time.

On that day, her old gray sofa welcomed us:

We sit on either end of the sofa, gathered into our flannel nightgowns. We breathe the warm steam from our mugs of hot cocoa. Funny how clearly this day looks in my memory, so far in the past it was. I had not thought about this day in many years. Just another scene from my soul's perambulation through time, I guess.

And Sarah starts:

"We flew all over the place when I was a kid. It was fun. I was never scared. Both my parents were pilots."

Sarah slurps a little cocoa.

"It was fun, Annette. We landed, hop-scotch, in every state. All the way, cross country. California to New York and back again. Three times we did it."

I look away, across the room at Sarah's wall of books. The morning sun glints on the hundreds of spines that jostle along all those shelves.

"Three times we went," says Sarah.

This is important. Let her talk. I take another sip of cocoa and Sarah continues with her story:

"My father had what he called his "flight cap." Maybe it was a talisman, Annette. I don't know. It was a sort of threadbare, black wool, baseball-style cap. The bill of the cap had been folded so many times, jammed into so many pants pockets, that all the stiffness had gone out of it. Along the crown there was a permanent crease going from what is eartop to eartop when it was on his head."

Another sip; we savor our steaming cocoas.

"He was never without his cap on our cross-country hops. We went through the South twice. Texas, Louisiana, Mississippi. You know. We'd fly at dawn to avoid the turbulent hot thermals. In the afternoons we'd tour the towns, walking all over the place under huge trees. Huge trees with hanging mosses. So different from our California trees. We'd walk into city halls. They all had those big red flags with fancy "Xs" on them. Our California flag has a bear in the center. Those red flags, every one of them, had this big "X" in the middle."

Sarah is looking to her left, gazing, as if seeing flags in the immediate distance.

"What we'd do in every town and city is get on a bus. We'd get right on, never knowing where we'd be going, and we'd ride the whole route, all the way to the bus terminal and then, chatting with the next bus driver as he came on duty, we'd ride all the way back to where we'd started."

"Y'all folks don't sit back there." The bus drivers would instruct us. All friendly like. "Y'all come up front with me."

"As we ride along, I see shacks made from crooked gray wood planks, and there were skinny little kids, and buckets flung empty on the ground in the yards, and hens were pecking around, and old women in drooping flowered dresses sometimes looked up at the bus as we went by. And our bus driver, fat, and the authority on the area, motions for us to look at this and that. From where I'm sitting behind him, I stare at his fat sunburnt neck as it rolls over the back of his gray bus uniform collar, and I see that his neck hairs are red and sprout out, all shorn and prickly, around his collar. I look out the bus window and see the big dusty trees. I see Nehigh Orange soda pop crates and a rusted American Flyer wagon in one yard, and broken pink dolls, headless, their plastic limbs flying. I am seven or eight or nine years old on these trips."

"That was back in the fifties, Sarah?" I had to say something.

"Yes, back then. We were not rich, Annette. It's not what you think. Having a little Cessna cost less back then than owning and maintaining a Chevy pickup now. I have snapshots of those trips, and in them my mother and I wore the same pedal pushers over several years of our travels. Mine started out mid-calf and ended up, several summers later, at my knees. And we stayed in cheap parking-lot motels with turquoise chlorine swimming pools. I loved those pools."

My mother and I wore the same pedal pushers over several years of our travels. Mine started out mid-calf and ended up, several summers later, at my knees.

Now it comes into view. Mrs. Zinn can see, at first through a slipstream of clouds, or is that the scrim on a stage? It lifts, and she sees as it comes into focus. It is Sarah's mother and father. It is a long time ago. They are planning another flight:

"How about we fly to Bishop?" He is asking, more like an order.

Sarah's mother replies:

"I suppose so. Yes. That's nice, dear."

"For some fishing?"

"Yeah, sure. Okay." Tentative.

Sarah's father continues:

"Since Sarah is away at school, we can take some time alone. Can't we? It's been forever."

Sarah's mother looks up at him from her wine glass. There is doubt. There is trust. Then doubt again, a twitch or a pucker – never a frown – at her left temple.

"You really want to do this, after . . ." She breaks off. Takes another sip of her wine.

His eyes slide up under his heavy lids. He takes her wine

glass and places it with a precise little click and a partial turn to straighten it along the near edge of the side table. He takes her hands, both of them, restraint as much as comfort for her.

He can charm a brick:

"You know how I feel," he says.

"Even after all that – you know – that thing with your secretary? You love me? Still?"

She looks up. Yes. She knows. She does know that. Now she knows. Yet, it's different. He has shifted. She can tell, and she says:

"Okay. Bishop. For fishing." she says, "It'll be fun." Gung-ho.

Then the lights go down on the scene just like on a stage in a community theatre, and the actors slip out in the dark, the stage creaking under their tiptoes, and the audience sits, rapt, waiting for the next scene to illuminate.

ow Annette is Sarah's witness. She sees Bishop now. Along the stream, Sarah's mother and father have flown up to Bishop in the Cessna. For fishing.

He flings his line, clumsy, annoyed, and it spins out in a useless flying loop, into the brush on the other bank.

He's talking now. A lecture. A litany:

"She was always, there. Always. We've never had a moment to ourselves. She's selfish and noisy. And her friends are stupid, and they giggle and, and, they're stupid. Why can't she ever just get a grip?"

Sarah's mother says:

"But I. But we wanted to have a baby. Now she's almost all grown up. College graduation is in a few days."

He is silent.

Sarah's mother continues:

"I was so happy when I found out I was pregnant. And even though you were thousands of miles away with the war and all, I was just so, just so happy. A part of you was with me. I never knew where you were. Where were you? Why can't you ever tell me? And she, she was so beautiful.

Little hands so tiny, and she could grip my fingers with all her tiny might."

"She was noisy. Always squirming. Always whining."

"No. She was just an infant. I loved her. I love her still."

"You." It is an exclamation.

He yanks in his line, jaw working. The line is tangled in twigs. There's even a torn old condom in the mess.

"You think I could just sit around waiting for her to grow up, so you and I could be alone? Do you? Do you? How do you think that feels?"

"But you love her, too. Don't you?"

"What choice did I have? The two of you, always together. And talk, talk, talk. Couldn't you ever just shut up? Couldn't she ever just get a grip?"

Well. Well.

I am not at all happy to have been given second sight, or insight, or whatever this three-day's adventure of my soul is, as it departs my body. I'm just an ordinary woman. Mrs. Annette Zinn. Seeing into the lives of my loved ones is too much for me to bear. It is too much. I want out.

Maybe that's the point: by the time you've seen your whole life pass before your very eyes, not to mention bits and pieces of the lives of your loved ones, by then, you will have had enough already, and you will go willingly, with gratitude even, into the world to come. Is that what the point of this life review is?

Okay maybe. Maybe not. But now the scene changes again, and I am going back into my own memories now.

*S*arah unfolds her legs, stretching, then flexing her bare toes she says to me:

"I loved those swimming pools."

She slurps a sip of tepid cocoa.

"Then we'd roll on out of the lives of the little Mississippi kids, eventually on to Texas, four days for crossing that enormous state, then New Mexico, sleep in Arizona, and home to the little airfield where we tied down. We'd make one pass all the way around the airstrip to make sure there weren't any other small planes taking off or landing – there was no such thing as an air traffic controller back then, especially at the little air fields where we landed. I'd look down into the trash chimneys that stood at the end of the landing strip. I loved seeing the bright red flames deep down in those chimneys. You know, I was never afraid."

We laugh a little, me at a joke I cannot comprehend, Sarah at her own childhood self perhaps. Then Sarah slips back into character as her childhood self:

"When we unlock the back door to our kitchen, the house smells stuffy. It's been shut tight for two weeks. Hot and still, the afternoon sun is stifled against the yellowing shades of our living room windows. My mother snaps them up, and they spin and flap as she lifts the lower pane of each window to let in the air and sunshine. My father takes off his flight cap, folds it neatly along its habitual crease, and flaps it onto the arm of the davenport."

I laugh. Can't help myself:

"They were 'davenports' long before they were 'sofas,' right Sarah!"

And we both laugh.

"My father, he's preoccupied. Sits there staring, silent. He got like that. Would just sit and stare. Not speak. Taking me to school one day, he just sits behind the steering wheel. Not talking. So, home again now, he looks over at me. His eyes – his irises, really – are tucked right up under his eyebrows. There's a half moon of white under each of his dark blue irises, and he says, distractedly, not seeing me really, and he says, not to me, really:

"Well, Sarah. You were always there. Always there."

Then he sighed. Tired, I guess. A sort of a groan really. And he had this thing he always did with his tongue behind his front teeth, a sort of sucking sound. And he got up and walked on down the hall. So. There we were, after one of our cross-country flights."

Sarah takes a sip of the cocoa dregs. Clunks her mug down, splashing a little cocoa on the table. She swipes at the spill with her palm and wipes her hand on her nightgown.

"I thought we'd been having fun." She said.

Well. Well.

Mary E. Carter

Again, Mrs. Zinn sees something: I am in the Cessna this time, flying back from the fishing expedition from Bishop. I am there as surely as if I had been there on that very day, at that very moment. Sarah's father is the pilot, and her mother is belted into her usual seat, co-pilot, beside him in the cabin. I do not want to see this scene. I do not want to be Sarah's witness. It is too much:

"I'm taking it down." Sarah's father announces.

He is a skilled pilot. Everything he does with the Cessna to keep it aloft is embedded in his synapses. He holds firm, hands gripping the opposite edges of the rectangular wheel. His body will fight the actions required to take the Cessna down. His body will act, reflexively, to keep the plane aloft:

"I'm taking us down."

This will take a perverse form of concentration on his part. This will be work. Counterintuitive. Deadly.

"I am taking us down."

He is the commander of his craft.

Sarah's mother sits there in her co-pilot posture, looking

straight ahead out over the nose of the plane, gripping her controls. The Cessna is heading down. It does not feel fast. She is surprised. It is slow, in slowest motion.

Sarah's father shouts:

"We're going down. It's all your. . ."

It stops. The scene breaks off.

I had to look away from Sarah then. I needed to look away from something that I had not known of, on that rainy day, sitting on Sarah's comforting old sofa. I had seen too much. I saw what had happened to Sarah. And that she could not, or would not, talk about it. Not then. I saw that too. This event in Sarah's life was to remain hidden, or forgotten even, from herself. I would not learn about it directly from her on that rainy day. That rainy day I turned away from Sarah, gazing out the big windows at the big bay.

Then there was more. A curtain lifts on the denouement: Sarah's parents have died in the crash of their Cessna. Tomorrow is Sarah's graduation day. I can see Sarah in those first moments after finding out about her parents' crash.

Sarah crosses the nighttime campus. Leaves rustle overhead, the sycamores. She has just left the dean's office. Why is she alone? Shouldn't someone escort her back to her dorm? But no. Nobody is with her. She walks, alone, back to her dorm to pack. She cannot think. She is in a dark state of anesthesia.

What could have happened to the Cessna? Sarah muses, ironic:

"Now I have my whole life ahead of me. Yes? What should I do?"

Call one of the boyfriends. Of course. Park with him a while. Wait out the storm. Sarah thinks:

"Here am I. I can go on, despite the odds. I guess they call them 'odds' because that is exactly what they are: Odd. I will never tell this story. To anybody. Ever. But I will know it. Forever."

*T*hen something else begins to unfold in front of Mrs. Zinn's eyes. Much against her will, she can suddenly see Sarah's future. The past was bad enough. But being flung into her future was to be even more disturbing:

Now, from my vantage point within the "hollow of the sling," I feel no joy at being gifted with precognition. Seeing into my beloved friend Sarah's life is hard. Seeing into her future is nothing I would have wished for. But I was about to experience a premonition of what would happen to Sarah many years from now.

I turn to look out at the bay. God knows there are fish in their millions out in those dark waters. Golden finned and bright-eyed; there is a world of living activity down there, sea creatures of all kinds. Purple, spiny puffer fish, lavender sea anemones, lazy flat fish, and maybe even a dappled octopus, flashing first purple, then orange, then magenta. So much life animates the deep waters in the bay, out there beyond Sarah's house.

Then I see into Sarah's future. What I see is this:

I am watching images projecting in front of my eyes like a movie trailer playing too loud with images flashing too fast. I am entranced. And the next feature is this:

Sarah will live to be a very old lady. Sarah will survive the discovery of her father's treachery. Piecing it all together, like a detective, Sarah will determine that it was a murder-suicide. In that way she will find out what happened in the Cessna. And, further still, I see that Sarah will be able to survive this excruciating knowledge. She will live. She will survive.

Out of nowhere, I remember Camus:

"There is but one truly serious philosophical problem, and that is suicide."

Sarah would become a person who would be the exact opposite of one who wants to end a life. We might take after our parents in ways they would never have intended. Sarah would become the opposite of her parents. Sarah would live on and on and on, despite the odds, despite what would appear to be the overwhelming odds that would confront her during her remaining lifetime. Odd.

Sarah would live on and on and on, despite the odds, despite what would appear to be the overwhelming odds that would confront her during her remaining lifetime. Odd.

Sarah never spoke to me again of flying after our rainy day on her sofa. Not ever.

How to fathom this. I do not know.

Mrs. Zinn wonders:

Is, was, this now, or then?
Am I, or was I, here, or there, then or now?
Was that then, or is this now?
Was that me, or is this me, now?
Where am, or was, I?
Is this now, or then, or when?
If not now, when?
I am, or was, so confused.
Am I here?
Or there?
Or where?
Is this now?
Or then?
Did this happen?
Or is this happening?
How can I see without having seen?
How now?
But not then?
I am so confused.
Was I always so confused?
Will I be thus, further, confused?
Where am I?
Here or there?
Or nowhere?
Am I lost?
Forgotten?
Both?
Neither?

Mrs. Zinn could see.
She could comprehend,
and she did.
It was a moment of lucid illumination:

Some children grow up to be
the exact opposite of their parents.

They can.

They will.

They do.

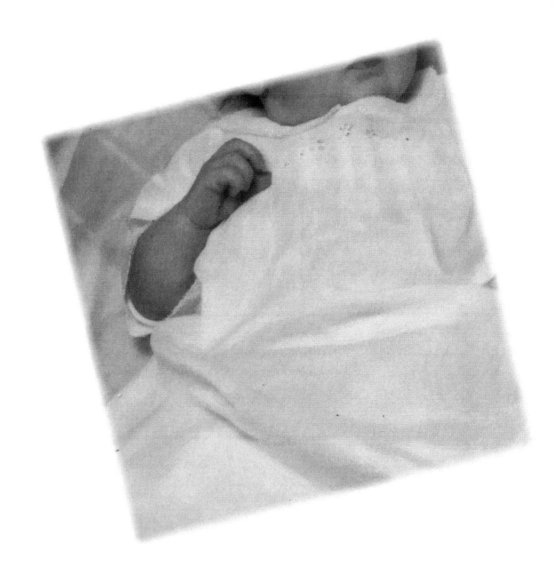

*Y*ou, the baby, do not remember the first major event of your life. Your birth. But, from her vantage point, heading for the world to come, Annette sees and experiences a mother's love, her mother's love for her. Her mother's love sufficed, even after she died, when Annette was twenty-two. Her mother's love sustained Annette for another 73 years.

Already beloved, I was born without much fuss as I, the baby, traveled along on my first trip of just a few inches and then into the daylight. My mother was made for having babies.

Already, as my blanket cocoon was delivered into her arms, at first sight of my little face nestling inside the flannel, my mother was in love. She was twenty-three. A wanted and desired baby, I landed in her arms, already her perfect little being – tu, tu, tu, as my grandmother Golda would say; do not tempt the devil with extravagant praise of the infant. There, there. There, and there, and here she is: your baby.

I will call her Annette; after her great Aunt Nettie.

I will call her Annette; after her great Aunt Nettie.

Now Mrs. Zinn is stepping into her mother's life, the life before there was an Annette. And she can see and perceive things and events that she could not possibly have experienced. Yet, these things and events are the essences, or the clay, that formed her, even before she knew she was being formed. Annette watched, as if watching a movie.

Was this, perhaps, what the kabbalists had named *"the hollow of a sling?"*

Now she can see into the times before her birth, her own birth. And her mother, Pearl, and her grandmother, Golda. And as much as you are born of people, so too you are born of a place and a time. Annette knew of her birth family, mother, father, grandparents, siblings, and bits and pieces of earlier generations. She realized now, at this backward review of her life, that she was formed as much of a location, that dot on a map, and of an era, that moment in time, as she was born of certain DNA. And, in fact, the locus of Mrs. Zinn's birth is perhaps even more influencing in her life than her genetic makeup.

But now, rather suddenly, this portion of the process of her soul's recollection speeds up for Annette. Now it is impossibly fast, a blizzard of images and events. It's like watching a newsreel that cuts from one event to another without an announcer to narrate the transitions. There seems to be no continuity to these latest recollections.

"There, but for fortune, go I."

She sees the photographs. She hears the stories. Her place on this earth has been, always, far removed from horrendous world events. The history of her birthplace was unmarked by war. No bombs destroyed the cities or the countryside. Thus, Annette learned:

"I am blessed."

She was blessed. Although, upon even hearing that word, "bless-ed," her grandmother would have forked her two first fingers outward pointing in a "V" shape, gesturing from her own lips, to fend off the evil eye, and she would have said:

"Tu, tu, tu."

It was the old-fashioned ladylike gesture meant to mimic

Her place on this earth has been, always, far removed from horrendous world events.

spitting at the devil. Do not invite bad luck with bragging, with overzealous praise, with loose talk.

It is now the evening of Day Two. Ere Day Three.

Quite a ride it has been, Mrs. Zinn. Yes?

She has watched her whole life spin madly, randomly, before her very eyes. She has seen and felt events in the lives of others. Quite a journey. Quite a wild ride. Now she perceives that she has a few slower moments in which to reconnoiter. Here is what Annette discovers:

Near the end of her life, my mother left me with her legacy.

"You have your whole life ahead of you, Netty."

And then Mrs. Zinn sees the precise moment when her mother had given her the legacy.

A blue bowl next to her mother's bed contains a peach, a banana, and an apple. The hot slow summer breeze blows gently over the slightly spoiled fruit. It fills the room with a sickly sweet scent. Her mother lies back against two rucked-up pillows. Weakened, weary, she slides slightly to her left. Her nightgown slips a little off her bony shoulder. She turns her face to Annette. Her eyes are large and brown and, unexpectedly, she looks young again and says:

"You have your whole life ahead of you, Annette."

"No, Mama. I do not have my life, *whole*, ahead of me."

But Annette did not say that. She did not say anything to her mother when her mother said the words:

"You have your whole life ahead of you."

Her mother had been twenty-three when she had had Annette. Annette was twenty-two when her mother died. Twenty-two when she, Annette Zinn, became a stranger in this strange land of life after death.

Annette, living on until she was ninety-five, after the loss of her mother, wandered in the diaspora of the survivors, and she would remain there, alone, for a very long time, indeed, for her whole life. Suddenly, poised on the edge of the world to come, Annette realizes:

"My mother has had more yahrzeits than birthdays."

It's true. But, think about it: almost everyone who has died will end up with more yahrzeits than birthdays. And Mrs. Zinn does consider that odd fact. She is still bobbing around overhead, but now more gently.

Think about it:

even if someone died yesterday, their yahrzeits will, eventually, outnumber their birthdays. Do the math. It's a compelling mathematical probability. Even if you are not very good at math. It is probably – no, it is definite –that, sooner or later, all the dead will end up with more yahrzeits than birthdays.

Going a step further: every single person previously alive on this earth will eventually have more yahrzeits than birthdays. It is one hundred percent probable. Probability is comforting, somehow.

Comforting?

Well, let's just say this: in our world, the one we live in now, before we enter the world to come – in a world like ours right now, one needs to take comfort where it may be found.

This is just a distraction, muses Annette. My attention flits around now. Now I want meaning, whatever that means.

What is the final conclusion for Mrs. Zinn, aged ninety-five and bound for whatever there is in the world to come?

Every single person previously alive on this earth will eventually have more yahrzeits than birthdays.

Things are slowing down at this point on the evening of Day Three. The documentary of Annette's life is slowly closing; roll credits.

Annette had of course heard, in the accounts of people who had had near-death experiences, for example, that there was a white light and a tunnel and a long ramp where all of one's loved ones, who had already gone into the world to come, would appear with emanations of love. Or some such. At ninety-five, when she set out on her own departure, that would mean that there would be quite a crush of people streaming toward her with love. Might it be a bit like a very crowded cocktail party? Annette never cared much for those kinds of huge social gatherings. Too many people. Too much distraction. Too scattered she had always been, with a bit of conversation here and two words shouted there. And although Annette had been very deft at "working the room" at parties, she had never really liked doing it. It was always exhausting.

Anyway, she was somewhat excited, and not a little bit anxious, too, anticipating this last moment, with its bright light and flowing love.

"You have your whole life ahead of you, Annette."

The power of her mother's dying words. But what had those words meant to Annette? How had those words influenced Annette?

"You have your whole life ahead of you, Annette."

Henry, Sarah, Grace, and Edie begin to recite kaddish. Mrs. Zinn sees the rabbi mingling with the other guests who are gathered around her gravesite. Was he invited? Was he summoned? Is he crashing my party? Is he being a helpful guide to me during my remaining time in "*the hollow of a sling*"? And look, over there, there's Milton. He looks so young. The gathering begins to recite Kaddish:

> *Exalted and hallowed be God's greatness*
> *In this world of Your creation.*
> *May Your will be fulfilled*
> *And Your sovereignty revealed*
> *And the life of the whole house of Israel*
> *Speedily and soon.*
> *And say, Amen.*

And there's Grace. She circulated, with grace, not drawing attention to herself. Just being there when required, with no fanfare, no need to be acknowledged. Grace, graceful and lovely, long-limbed, straight-spined, doing what needed to be done, standing beside Annette's dark grave,

*May Your
will be fulfilled…
Speedily
and soon.*

holding a little shovel in her steady hands – with grace.

May You be blessed forever,
Even to all eternity.
May You, most Holy One, be blessed,
Praised and honored, extolled and glorified,
Adored and exalted above all else.

And Edie. Edie always late, shouting hello, but not today. Beloved crazy and adored Edie, standing still and silent today beside the deep, deep hole into which her beloved friend, Annette Zinn, would venture into the world to come.

Blessed are You.
Beyond all blessings and hymns, praises and consolations
That may be uttered in this world,
In the days of our lifetime,
And say, Amen.

And here is Sarah. Sarah, now in her forties, is just beginning to wake up to the idea of the world to come. So many of Sarah's days of her lifetime had been in conversation with Annette, wandering in free-association, in reconstruction of their similar pasts. Decades they had

May You
be blessed forever.

together, piecing their lives together, mending their broken places – members of that same club – the club nobody else wanted to belong to. Motherless daughters.

Annette knows what Sarah is thinking:

"You finally get it all together and then you just die? That's just not fair, God! That's not fair."

Sarah Sax, as in saxophone, is now Sarah Steinway, as in piano. She stands on the very edge of the dark, deep rectangle, dug, now, into the earth. This is where Annette will venture into the world to come. Sarah looks into the earthen bed:

"Oh, God, whoever you may be – he, she, or it – if you are there, or here, or any-damn-where, make her memory be for a blessing."

> *May peace abundant descend from heaven*
> *With life for us and for all Israel,*
> *And Say, Amen.*
> *May God, who makes peace on high,*
> *Bring peace to all and to all Israel,*
> *And say, Amen.*

May God...
bring peace to all.

Henry Preston steps forward to the edge of the gravesite. And if he is weeping, it is only evident by three muffled throat-clearing sounds and several squeaky gulps from beneath his tallis.

Henry is wondering:

"If I had been able to find peace in Mrs. Zinn's presence, was it by sheer luck or was this mere happenstance? How had I been so lucky? Tu, tu, tu."

Yet, now, sadness as the friends gather, with more life still ahead of them, but forever after, without their friend, Annette.

Henry recalls a question that was debated in the Talmud:

When a funeral procession and a bridal procession meet at a crossroads, which one should go first?

The rabbis decided that life should always take precedence. And so, the bridal procession crosses first, then the funeral procession.

In the background of this gathering, Annette sees the rabbi. He's working the room it seems, not that he's actually engaging anyone in small talk. But Annette knows this is just for her; nobody else can perceive his presence on this, Day Three, of Mrs. Zinn's departure. She is reminded:

> *"In the corpus of Jewish mystical literature, it is said that for three days after the death of the body, the soul is still hovering close to the body, so to speak, and does not completely depart from it. In short, the soul requires some time to accustom itself to its new situation."*

Annette wishes that she had paid more attention to the book, *The Soul*. She would have been more prepared for what has been happening. This movie, or whatever it was, this newsreel, with scenes cutting back and forth in time and in space and zooming in on first this person and then on that person – it has been dizzying. It has been confusing. At times, it has been upsetting.

Another memory floods in, this time a quote from the book, *The Soul*, reminding Annette that:

> *"After the soul departs from the body, it undergoes a process of rectification . . . this process is known in the*

kabbalistic literature as the 'hollow of a sling.' Simply put, this is the most comprehensive overview possible of our lives in this world; it is similar to the old saying that 'when you die, your whole life passes before your eyes.'

. . . In the 'hollow of a sling,' by contrast, the soul . . . apprehends the whole of its former life process at once . . . The soul acquires a certain comprehension of the details of events that were **forgotten or hidden** *during its time in this world."*

Then again, with an ear to sub-text, Mrs. Zinn cannot resist a question. She perceives a sub-text in this book.

"But, Rabbi, I have a question."

And there he is: another vision appearing before Mrs. Zinn with his kippah, his long white scholar's beard. His presence was more than just that of her imagination. Was he actually appearing here in the world to come, yet another character in her own "bird's eye view" of her own life? Could she actually see him, right now, sitting behind his massive workroom table, leaning on his own elbow, hand to brow, sighing and murmuring at her temerity.

"Oy!"

"But listen, Rabbi," she says:

"While you have written extensively about death, and the soul, and whatnot, I must ask you: do you actually agree with these spiritual concepts and notions? Or are you simply recording these various theories for the reader, for me, to consider? In other words, Rav, do you actually *believe* in these things?"

And, again, she hears him say:

"Oy!"

If only she could write him a letter to ask about his true feelings. Yet, as in all things Torah, and certainly as in all things kabbalistic, there is much room for debate. Witness the commentary, some of it centuries old. And let's also acknowledge that even Annette Zinn, a secular Jew, is entitled to, and even encouraged, to think for herself.

"Do you actually believe, Rabbi, that there are three days for the 'hovering of the soul' after death?"

No response, learned or otherwise.

"If this is true, Rabbi, then is this – this thing I have experienced – has this been my three days of hovering?"

If only she had paid more attention in the many classes and lectures that she had attended over the years. For Annette, those classes had been more about socializing with her widowed friends and sampling the yummy home-made sweets at the oneg. She was that lacking in scholarship. All temporal, she would say, tapping her own forehead. Secular and of this world, was Mrs. Zinn.

Let us imagine, no, assume, that there was a great white light at the last moment of Mrs. Zinn's departure. Maybe not the ramp. No. Scratch the ramp. But in this moment of white light, let's posit that Annette could finally see what her life had been. It was so simple, so obvious to her now. It was her mother's legacy:

"You have your whole life ahead of you, Netty."

While she had had, for decades, thought that her mother's legacy to her had been to survive in spite of not being whole. Clearly, no. Her mother's legacy to her had been life itself. Of course. Hidden in the words of her own mother had been the word *life.* Contained within her mother's last words was the word "life." Simple. Her mother's words contained life. The message was not necessarily about making life *whole.*

Life.

Simple.

Even the Kaddish invokes only life and never mentions death.

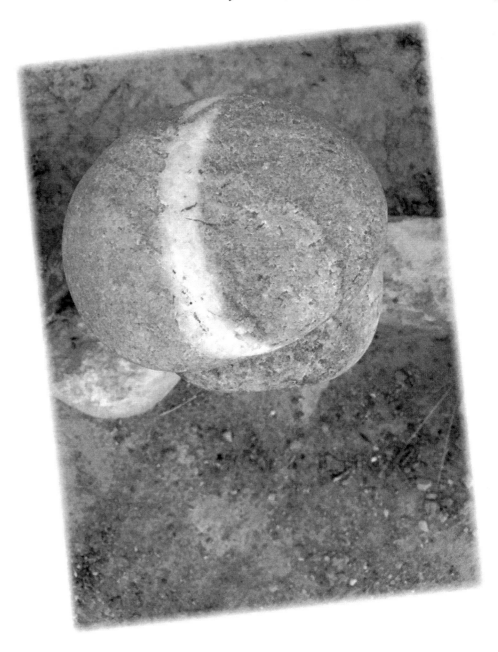

And so, Mrs. Zinn, what do you finally comprehend about your life?

Yes, she wonders: what were my themes?

Retreat vs. engagement? Attachment vs. aversion – very yogic, that one. Attachment to beauty? To cherished friends? Or how about this – life includes what we know and what we do not know, things hidden and forgotten along with all the things we remember. Well, that's pretty mundane isn't it? There's nothing very world-shaking in any of these conclusions.

She has one last question:

"Where's my epiphany? I feel cheated, a little. So, I get my Three Days, but no epiphany? I was expecting something more grand. After all, I have had ninety-five years of living life. Where's the big sendoff? I want my epiphany! I want spectacle!"

Annette looks around her – takes in her beloved friends, past and present:

"What can I say to them in conclusion? So: what's it all about, Alfie? We are only human. We want answers."

She sees into the souls of Henry and of Sarah and of Grace and Edie. And here, hovering around the edges of this gathering, this leave-taking, there is Milton and her parents, and his parents, and a few other souls wearing shtreimels, dimly lit in the background. Who are they she wonders?

"You know what, Rabbi? You know how we always say after the death of a loved one, we say, 'may her memory be a blessing?' Well, you know what, Rav? After these three days of my departure, I would rather that people say to me, right to my face, and let's hope just moments before my end, I want people to say to me:

"May your memories be a blessing."

"See what I mean, Rabbi? I would rather hear people say to me:

"May your memories, revealed along with all the things that had been either hidden or forgotten, may those memories be, for you, the blessing."

Then it dawns on her: if you want your epiphanies, if you want your sure things, ask a fundamentalist. No matter which religion – even the atheists – they all talk about death and life as if they, alone, have the answers to how it all works. Heaven, that's what awaits. No, no! It's Hell. No, no, no.

It's nothing. "Nothing," says the atheist, loud and clear. See. Even the atheists believe in something. Only, their something is No Thing.

Everybody is so damn sure when the only sure thing is that there is NO sure thing.

"I have never understood how so many atheists could write so many books, and articles, and essays. It's a wonder how they could make so much out of No Thing."

Well and well.

enry repeats the words:

>*May peace abundant descend from heaven*
>*with life for us . . .*

Mrs. Annette Zinn – A-Double-N, E-Double-T-E – is not sad at the sight of her own deep grave. It is Day Three. She is not sad at all. And, certainly, she is not at all afraid.

It is Shiva – back at Annette's house. A house full of everyone. The people from the "Y" and from the Homeless Women's Shelter. They are all longtime friends now. Old friends. And younger friends, too, are here. Dozens. All have been, at one time or another, embraced, or enabled, by Mrs. Annette Zinn. All of them.

Annette bobs gently, up by the ceiling. She sees herself below. She is seated in her usual chair in her library. At this point, she is almost wholly departed from the company that is flowing around her room. She can neither speak nor act upon any of these activities.

The draperies shift on a warm breeze, a soft breath, then stillness. She is detached. She is gone and done with her life. She has departed.

She is seated
in her usual chair
in her library.

Henry places a single folded napkin swan on her chair. And he whispers:

"May her memory be – as it always was for me – a blessing."

Look at her: Mrs. Annette Zinn.
See that she is an ordinary woman.
She has had three days to review – to view again – her life.
Her ninety-five years.
Ninety-five seasons of sunshine and rain and wind and some
eclipses of the sun or of the moon.
And people and events and those she loved
and those she could not love;
she has had three days to view these again.
One life. Such a long one. An ordinary life.
Not too many bad things.
Very many good things.
Throughout it all, she was doing the best she could.
Only human.
Absolutely human.
Facing her destination.
May her memory be.
Just be.

AFTERWORD: SARAH

My name is Sarah Steinway. As in piano. I first met Annette Zinn about twenty-five years ago. Maybe it was more. I lose count. She and Henry Preston were regulars at the Bullock's Tea Room. I guess that means I met them both back then. Back then I was the Napkin Girl. That was me, Sarah Sax, as in saxophone. It was a part-time job for me while I attended graduate school after the deaths of my parents. Actually, I had two part-time jobs back then. Busy, busy. A high-functioning neurotic I was, despite my parents dying in the Cessna, just a day before my college graduation.

Now that Shiva's done, I am ready to go back home. No more flying back and forth to see Annette and Henry. I am ready to stay home with Daniel. Forever. No more leaving our home high above the San Pablo Bay. Henry plans to travel for a while, and he will keep in touch. Will he, though?

Daniel and I share our home with shore birds. They nest among the reeds, and we watch their flocks gather at sunset

along the bay to the east.

I loved Annette Zinn. Oh, God knows we quarreled. There were misunderstandings like any other friendship. There is one time I remember. We were just sitting, chatting about this and that:

"Sarah, I just don't like your new paintings."

"Oh?"

"Bizarre naked, pregnant figures. Are they birds? Are they human beings? Wings flapping all over the place. Why can't you just stick to your folded napkins?"

"Annette! Why should I?"

"Well, that's just it, Sarah. Everybody loves your napkin animals."

"So? So, I should always make what people love? It's a popularity contest? Is that what you think art is?"

Annette shrugged her left shoulder and picked out a piece of rye bread. Favoring her new manicure, she pulled a morsel away from its crust – a sign that she was changing tack:

"You never talk about . . ."

I interrupt:

"No, Annette. No. Yes, you're right. I do not talk about my parents."

"Sarah-la."

"Mrs. Zinn."

"A-Double-N, E-Double-T-E."

"I know, Annette. I know. But not now. I'm not ready."

Annette placed her small manicured fist against her chest, then drawing it away from her heart, she made three small thumps, almost imperceptible, making amends, I think, for pushing me too far this time. And I knew she loved me. And I loved her. Words fail.

When I got back home from Annette's funeral, Daniel was waiting with two glasses of wine. We went over to our two big east-facing windows, watching our sunset in reverse. We are the eyes of our Taliesin home.

A sip of wine as we watch this day end:

"To Annette."

"May her memory be for a blessing."

Mrs. Zinn is gone and done with life. We sip, two little sips and gaze out to the east, watching the traces of the sun setting behind us, ending this day, sip by sip.

Down below us there, in the shallow wetlands, three white egrets tiptoe through the pink reeds. The water comes up to their knees, if such knobs may be called knees. They pick their way along the incoming tide, stretching their necks forward to find footholds in the wet sand. They are shore birds, white as white, and the water, deepening now, is black.

We clink our glasses:

To Life! L'Chaim!

—END—

—ACKNOWLEDGMENTS—

Thank you to the editor at the Faber Academy who provided me with two full manuscript reviews.

Thank you to my dear friend and line editor, Allison Wilkes Smith.

Thank you to Rabbi Steinsaltz, and to his publishers for allowing me to include excerpts from *The Soul*.

Thank you to the publishers for allowing me to include a quote from Robert Alter's *The Hebrew Bible, Volume 3*.

Thank you, Rabbi Jack Shlachter, for discerning, and naming, the pintele yid in all my characters.

Thank you Gary W. Priester, husband of more than forty years and best friend ever, for graphic design and type for this beautiful book.

I have made this story in remembrance of my friends: Bea and Joel. Did this story really happen? They did not know one another on this side of the world to come. If they had met, perhaps this story could have been non-fiction.

Mary E. Carter
Placitas, New Mexico, USA

—Book List—

The Soul by Rabbi Adin Even-Israel Steinsaltz, Maggid Books, an Imprint of Koren Publishers Jerusalem Ltd., 2018

Saying Kaddish by Anita Diamant, Shocken Books, New York, 1998

The Hebrew Bible: Translation with Commentary by Robert Alter, W. W. Norton & Company, Inc., 2019

—About the Type—

The primary text in this book is set in Sabon MT. Sabon is an old-style serif typeface designed by the German-born typographer and designer Jan Tschichold in the period 1964–1967. It was released jointly by the Linotype, Monotype, and Stempel type foundries in 1967.

The lovely initial caps are formatted in Arial Bold Pro from the Argentina Lián Types Foundry, created in 2008 by Maximiliano Sproviero. Maximiliano loves typography and was interested in the beauty of it when he started studying Graphic Design at Universidad de Buenos Aires, Argentina.

Mrs. Zinn's musings are set in Raleway Extra Light.

The floral flourish at the start of the text sections is from Pushenko. Visun Khankasem provided the elegant flourishes at the end of each text section. Both are represented by ShutterStock.com

—Message to the Reader From the Author—

The first questions I hear, after someone has read my fiction, are these:

"Did this really happen? Did this happen to you?"

These questions can launch a longer discussion than most discerning readers could actually tolerate, having just put down my novel.

But, I'm game; so here goes.

The answers are yes and no. Or, no and yes. Or something in between. I equivocate. I dodge. Reluctant to be pinned down, and fearful of being misunderstood, I hedge.

Yes, I do ransack my own experiences for "material." No, I do not simply copy them down. I do not simply take dictation from my own life and its events. I, rather, make of my own life and my own experiences, a kind of reduction sauce. I cook and cook and lower the flame and let things bubble and reduce everything down, and add a little of this and a little of that, all in the hope of making a tastier concoction.

For example:

I could take a quarter pound of butter and a cup of heavy cream and a whole unpeeled garlic and an onion and a handful of pink peppercorns and a slab of filet mignon and fling them, all at once, directly at you, and it would be quite a mess. It might even cause injury. I prefer to soften the onion in a bit of sizzling butter and then add a morsel of crushed garlic and turn down the heat and slowly let the butter and the onion and the garlic meld into a flavor that is not of any single component, but that is an entirely new flavor. Then if I drizzle in some of the cream, and stir it around with a wooden spoon that belonged to my mother, and if I then offer you a lovely crystal goblet of *Sancerre*, and we savor it while standing in my kitchen, and if we talk about when we were kids back in the sixties – well, then, you see – now those ingredients might make something very tasty.

It is the same with making my own life experiences into fiction. A bit of this. A little of that. Let it cook – slowly – stir it up a little and, eventually, it makes a story.

And what is fact? And what is fiction? There is fact in fiction. And much fiction in fact; so we are told. So where to draw the line? If Mrs. Annette Zinn is the heroine in her own story, what is, in fact, her story? If Mrs. Annette Zinn is formed of the imagination of another person, does that make her story more, or less, true? If Mrs. Annette Zinn is the personification of many women who lived, in real life, then, what parts of her story are fiction—in that they represent the stereotypes of many such women? And what parts in her story are fact?

Am I Mrs. Zinn? Is Mrs. Zinn me?

When facts read like plots from the greatest fiction, does that mean that those facts are fiction, mere fantasies? When fiction reads like life, real-life, does that make it any less true?

Mary E. Carter
Placitas, New Mexico
USA

Made in the USA
San Bernardino, CA
26 July 2019